Cat turned to see Nick  with Zak. 'We need a ─── said. 'And it's got to start ─────── ─── N.A.

'I've got it!' Nick shouted, punching the air. 'Nick's Angels!'

'Nick's Angels?' Cat laughed as Belle emitted a very uncool, un-Belle-like snorting sound that was somewhere between horror and amusement.

'We are certainly not *your* angels!' Belle scoffed

'Yeah. We're *nobody's* angels, thank you very much!' Cat said, poking Nick in the ribs.

Then she suddenly stopped laughing, replaying what she had just said in her head.

She looked at Holly and Holly looked at Belle. There was a long freeze-frame pause and then . . .

'That's it!' Holly said.

'We're Nobody's Angels!' all three girls shouted in unison.

www.kidsatrandomhouse.co.uk

Also available in the Superstar High series:

THE TIME OF YOUR LIFE

Superstar HIGH

WHERE YOUR DREAMS COME TRUE

NOBODY'S ANGELS

Isabella Cass

CORGI BOOKS

SUPERSTAR HIGH: NOBODY'S ANGELS
A CORGI BOOK 978 0 552 56076 4

Published in Great Britain by Corgi Books,
an imprint of Random House Children's Books
A Random House Group Company

This edition published 2009

1 3 5 7 9 10 8 6 4 2

Special thanks to Helen Moss

Series created and developed by Amber Caravéo
Cover illustration by Jerry Paris
Copyright © Random House Children's Books, 2009

All rights reserved. No part of this publication may be reproduced,
stored in a retrieval system, or transmitted in any form or by any means,
electronic, mechanical, photocopying, recording or otherwise, without
the prior permission of the publishers.

The Random House Group Limited supports the Forest Stewardship
Council (FSC), the leading international forest certification organization.
All our titles that are printed on Greenpeace-approved FSC-certified
paper carry the FSC logo. Our paper procurement policy can be found at
www.rbooks.co.uk/environment

Set in Bembo
by Falcon Oast Graphic Art Ltd.

Corgi Books are published by Random House Children's Books,
61–63 Uxbridge Road, London W5 5SA

www.**kids**at**randomhouse**.co.uk
www.**rbooks**.co.uk

Addresses for companies within The Random House Group Limited
can be found at: www.randomhouse.co.uk/offices.htm

THE RANDOM HOUSE GROUP Limited Reg. No. 954009

A CIP catalogue record for this book is available from the British Library.

Printed and bound in Great Britain by CPI Bookmarque, Croydon, CR0 4TD

For Grandma

CHAPTER ONE

Holly: Dreams, Puddles and Louis Vuitton

Holly Devenish had dreamed of this moment all her life.

Well, perhaps not this *precise* moment — she was wrestling her backpack out of the boot of the taxi — but for twelve years, four months and seventeen days she had dreamed of arriving to start her first term at stage school.

Even thinking the words *stage school* sent a thrill of excitement rippling down her spine.

And it wasn't just *any* stage school. The Garrick School of the Performing Arts in central London was only the most famous, the oldest, the generally-all-round-coolest-and-best stage school in the country, if not in the known universe. No wonder people called it . . . Superstar High. The Garrick had produced enough stars to fill a whole new galaxy!

As she gazed up at the grand school building, the rose-coloured brickwork glowing softly in the

September sunshine, Holly could still hardly believe her luck. If Miss Toft, her dance coach since she was a toddler in a tutu, hadn't secretly entered her for the 'Steps to the Stars' competition, this would never have been possible. The judging panel had included two dance teachers from the Garrick, and the prize was a scholarship to the famous school. The Garrick didn't admit students until Year Eight; so today Holly was just one of eighty twelve- and thirteen-year-old students arriving to begin their first year – and their new life – at Superstar High.

The backpack was wedged firmly against a holdall full of dance shoes and was refusing to budge. Mum had disappeared through the imposing double front doors of the school to let them know that Holly had arrived, and the taxi driver was nowhere to be seen. It was an enormous backpack – the kind a family of four might take for a month-long camping trip to Outer Mongolia. At a pinch, they'd probably be able to camp *in* the backpack.

Summoning up every ounce of strength in her petite, fine-boned frame, Holly grabbed the shoulder strap with both hands and gave an enormous heave.

'*Yes!*' she shouted as the backpack shot out of the boot and over her shoulder.

And crash-landed in a puddle the size of a small lake. *SPLASH!*

'*Eeeuuu-arggghhhh!*'

The sound was a cross between the dying squawk of a strangled parrot and the mating cry of a howler monkey. Hardly daring to look, Holly turned round.

On the far side of the puddle stood a matching set of luggage in soft beige leather: three suitcases, a vanity case and two hat-boxes. Muddy water was polka-dotted across every single one of them.

Not to mention the cream suede boots of their owner.

Very slowly Holly lifted her eyes from the boots to the face of the girl wearing them: a tall girl with ruler-straight blonde hair cut into a sharp bob. Her eyes were the cold blue of a gas flame. There was only one word to describe her expression: furious.

'I – I'm so sorry. It – it just came off in my hand . . .' Holly stammered, staring at the torn strip of canvas still clenched in her fist. She couldn't believe it! She'd been determined to leave her clumsiness behind when she started at the Garrick, and here she was, in the running for the Klutz of the Year award before she'd even got in the door!

'Sorry? Oh, you *will* be,' Furious Girl spat. 'That's *Louis Vuitton*!'

'Oh no! Where?' Holly gasped, looking round to see who else she had managed to drench. Then she realized the girl was referring to her designer suitcases. She felt a blush begin to creep across her face; although her skin was a dark caramel shade, she knew it wouldn't hide the fact that she was entering tomato territory.

'I don't suppose you have *any* idea how much this luggage *costs*,' Furious Girl snapped, 'but I'll be sending you the cleaning bill, you stupid, clumsy little—'

An even taller girl suddenly stepped out of a gleaming black Mercedes. She had golden hair in two long plaits under a black beret that was perfectly plain but somehow had *style* written all over it. She removed her designer sunglasses, took a sip from her bottle of mineral water and sized up the situation. 'Hey, girl, lucky they're only last year's design!' Style Girl spoke with the kind of punchy New York accent Holly recognized from American TV shows. 'Now, if it was *this* season's collection, I can see how you might be a *teensy* bit mad about it!'

'Yeah, *right*! Like you'd know what this season's Louis Vuitton looks like!' Furious Girl snarled. 'It's not even in the shops yet!'

Style Girl smiled and swept a perfectly manicured hand towards the tiny vanity case she was towing behind her. She stepped aside to reveal a set of matching luggage being stacked into a teetering mountain by a uniformed chauffeur and a large man in a brown cord suit and a turban. *So that's where my taxi driver got to*, Holly thought.

Holly wouldn't honestly have known the difference between this season's Louis Vuitton and last season's Topshop, but the look on Furious Girl's face left her in no doubt: the luggage mountain was the genuine article.

Raising one eyebrow a fraction, Style Girl smiled at Holly. 'Hello, how're you? I'm Belle Madison,' she said with a friendly, if slightly formal, handshake. Turning graciously towards Furious Girl, she held out her hand again. 'And you are . . .'

But the owner of last season's luggage had vanished.

'. . . really quite annoyed!' Holly answered on her behalf.

Belle grinned. She turned to the taxi driver and waved a ten-pound tip in front of his nose. He and the Mercedes' chauffeur scooped up the suitcases and staggered after her.

Holly watched in hushed admiration.

'Bianca Hayford,' said a voice.

'Er, sorry?' Holly muttered, suddenly noticing a

pretty red-haired girl, who was trying to lift Holly's marooned backpack out of the puddle.

'The drama-queen you just showered with muddy water,' the girl said. 'Her name's Bianca Hayford.'

'Er, is she a friend of yours?' Holly asked.

'Oh, now, do I look like I'd have a friend who only uses *last year's* Louis Vuitton?' the girl replied. Then she threw back her head, catching sparks of sunshine in her flame-red curls, and laughed a bubbling, throaty laugh. 'Just kidding!' she said. 'I saw the name tags on those fancy designer bags of hers.'

This girl is seriously glamorous, Holly thought, gazing at her new friend, who was wearing a figure-hugging black 1950s dress, a fake-fur wrap and leather biker boots. *What's more, she actually has a figure for the dress to hug!* Holly thought enviously. She couldn't help glancing down at her own slim frame in its white T-shirt and skinny jeans. It was far from curvy!

'Well, come on then. Let's get your bag out of this puddle. Oh – my name's Cat. Catrin Wickham, if you want to be posh!' Cat spoke in a soft Irish accent. As she heaved at the backpack, drops of water flicked from it onto her dress and she broke out into that danger-ously infectious laugh again. '*Eau de Puddle!* Everyone's wearing it this season!' she said.

Holly couldn't help laughing as she held out her hand politely and introduced herself. But Cat leaped across the puddle and engulfed her in a great big hug. Holly hugged her back. Usually she felt a little shy and awkward when she met new people, but somehow shyness didn't seem to be an option with Cat!

'Great to see you're making friends already!' Holly's mum called as she emerged from the school building.

And enemies! Holly thought, thinking of Furious Girl and hoping she wouldn't be running into her again for a very long time.

Somehow she didn't think she'd made it onto Bianca Hayford's Christmas card list.

CHAPTER TWO

Holly: Welcome to Superstar High!

'This is Lucy Cheng,' Holly's mother said, smiling as she introduced a slim Chinese girl in a tracksuit who'd followed her down the steps. 'She's in Year Ten here – she's going to look after you.'

Then, with a quick hug and a mumbled 'Love you,' she turned away to hide her tears and hurried back to the taxi. For a moment Holly longed to run after her – she'd never been away from home for more than a week before, let alone to boarding school, and she felt a little scared. But then she glanced at the flight of steps leading up to the front door. Each one was flanked by a pair of tiny trees in clay pots, expertly pruned into star shapes. *The Steps to the Stars!* Holly thought. She had worked so hard to get here. Dancing was her life!

The excitement was like a swarm of bees trying to burst out of her ribcage, and all thoughts of going home with her mum vanished. She knew she was right where she wanted to be.

'Ooh, can I come with you and see your room?' Cat asked. 'I've been here since the crack of dawn!' She chatted non-stop as they dragged Holly's bags up the steps. 'I can't wait to meet my roommate; she hasn't arrived yet. I wonder who you'll be sharing with . . .'

Holly followed Lucy and Cat into a huge, elegant entrance hall. The rich tones of the oak-panelled walls were highlighted by shafts of golden sunlight flooding through the high windows, which followed the curve of a grand, sweeping staircase to the floors above. Armchairs were clustered around coffee tables strewn with magazines. A group of students in Victorian costumes were sitting talking about a film shoot, while others poured themselves drinks from a watercooler in the corner. On the other side of the hallway there was a reception area, with pigeonholes, notice boards and a big old-fashioned desk.

And everywhere Holly looked, people were bustling purposefully from place to place, up and down the stairs, in and out of corridors, some carrying instrument cases, others with spotlights or microphones. The soundtrack was the *clatter-chatter-buzz* of shared activity.

Two girls in sweats and legwarmers were leaning on the banister doing quad-stretches while a third was talking into a mobile phone. Holly caught the spine-tingling words *audition* and *casting* and she couldn't wait to be part of it! She was crazy about all forms of dance – from classical ballet to Irish folk dancing – and she loved singing too. Her dream was to play starring roles in big West End and Broadway musicals – Roxy Hart in *Chicago*, Sandy in *Grease*, Baby in *Dirty Dancing* and this place, Superstar High, was her big chance!

Holly snapped out of her daydream as Lucy led her over to the reception desk, which was manned by a plump lady with a helmet of tightly curled white hair. She was sitting in a large, important-looking black leather swivel chair, and the name-badge on the lapel of her red–and–mauve–checked trouser suit announced that she was MRS N. A. BUTTERWORTH, SCHOOL SECRETARY.

'Hello, dear, welcome to the Garrick.' Mrs Butterworth smiled at Holly, patting her ample tartan-armoured chest with both hands as she reached for the glasses hanging on a gold chain around her neck. She settled the glasses on the tip of her powdered nose and peered over them at the computer screen. 'Devenish . . . Devenish . . . Ah yes, here we are. Room twenty-five!'

'Brilliant! That's next door to me,' Cat declared.

Before Holly could say anything, Mrs Butterworth suddenly swivelled her chair out from behind the desk and, with a quick shove, scooted halfway across the hall. 'Felix Baddeley! Ethan Reed!' she bellowed. 'Get over here, you big lardy lumps! Help this little lass upstairs with her bags!'

Two of the Victorian students hurried across to the desk, where Mrs Butterworth had returned to her position of command. She was obviously not a woman to be disobeyed. The boys grinned as they stood to attention and saluted.

The one Mrs Butterworth had addressed as Felix was sporting a Sherlock-Holmes-style cape, and a deer-stalker hat over a tangle of dreadlocks. The other, Ethan, was wearing breeches and a waistcoat. He reached up and peeled a bushy old-fashioned beard from his jaw. A *very* attractive jaw, Holly couldn't help noticing, in spite of the red marks left by the beard-glue. He had short dark hair, sea-green eyes, and a slightly lopsided smile.

'Ooh, he *smiled* at you, Holly,' Cat whispered, nudging Holly's elbow as they followed Lucy and the boys up several flights of stairs.

'Sshh! He'll hear you,' Holly told her. 'Anyway, he was just being polite. He smiled at everyone equally!'

'Some of us,' Cat said with a grin, 'more *equally* than others!'

'Here we are,' Lucy announced. '*Home sweet home!* Complete with Shreddie, the school cat,' she added, pointing to a colossal marmalade cat sitting like a security guard outside room twenty-five.

Holly stooped to tickle Shreddie's soft golden ears and then pushed open the door.

The light, cosy room was decorated in white and primrose, with cheerful yellow and orange accessories. The two beds were covered with cushions and throws, and beside each one was a study area with a bookshelf and desk, complete with an angle-poise lamp and a pile of fat new textbooks. The centre of the room contained a collection of beanbags, a sheepskin rug and a round coffee table topped by a vase of sunflowers.

Light flooded into the room from one large window, and sitting in the window seat, a tall girl in a white dressing gown was towel-drying her blonde hair, her feet resting on a small beige suitcase.

'Hey, *Belle*!' Holly called out, delighted that her roommate was someone she'd already met.

But the girl who looked up was not the ultra-cool and friendly American who'd rescued her from the unfortunate puddle-bomb incident. There was no mistaking those glacier-blue eyes.

Holly was sharing a room with . . .

Bianca Hayford.

CHAPTER THREE

Cat: A Lucky Escape

Cat watched in horror as Bianca fixed Holly with her icy stare.

'Oh, no, not Little Miss Clumsy!' Bianca said.

There was one of those long silences where everyone exchanges *significant* looks. At least, they do in films. In reality, Cat noticed, people usually just stared at their feet. Holly was *totally* mesmerized by her shoes right now! Just when it was starting to get really uncomfortable, Holly lifted her chin and stepped forward with a brave smile. 'Bianca, I'm sorry about your bags,' she said quietly, 'but it was an accident. Could you just get over it so that we can be friends?'

Wow! Holly is tougher than she looks, Cat thought. *She's like Maria in* The Sound of Music. Cat knew she would've *died* if she'd had to share with Bianca. Or thrown a hissy fit and demanded to switch rooms.

Confusion flickered across Bianca's face. She clearly wasn't used to people standing up to her. 'Well . . . just make sure it doesn't happen again. Oh, and two more things,' she added. 'First thing: *my* side – *your* side.' She gestured at the two halves of the room like an air stewardess indicating the emergency exits. 'Don't cross the line!'

Cat felt anger sizzling up inside her. Who did Bianca think she was, talking to Holly like that? She opened her mouth to protest.

'And the second thing?' Holly asked calmly, before Cat could get a word out.

'Don't let that cat in here!' Bianca hissed.

For a moment Cat thought that Bianca had singled her out for special attack. Then she realized that the other girl was pointing at Shreddie, who had nosed his way into the room.

'I have *allergies*!' Bianca explained.

Cat scooped Shreddie up and snuggled her chin into his fur. 'Come on, mate. Some people just don't appreciate us . . . See you later!' she mouthed to Holly, stepping gratefully out of the room. It seemed that Holly was more than capable of dealing with Bianca by herself!

When Cat pushed open the door of her own room next door a moment later, she did a double-take – and almost dropped Shreddie. It was the blonde-girl-plus-Vuitton-luggage combo all over again – except *this* blonde girl was standing on her head. 'Er, what are you doing?' Cat asked.

'*Sirsha-asana*,' the upside-down girl said.

Uh-oh, Cat thought. *Holly got the mean one, but I got the crazy one!*

'Yoga,' said the girl, lowering her legs. 'It's very relaxing.'

Cat recognized Belle Madison, the just-stepped-out-of-American-*Vogue* girl who'd saved Holly from the Wrath of Bianca.

Belle smiled warmly. 'Hey, roomy. Great to meet you!'

Cat grinned back and glanced around the room. Belle had already unpacked a shiny new laptop, a small electric keyboard, a mini-fridge and, most importantly, an enormous box of Belgian chocolates which was sitting on the coffee table.

'Welcome to room twenty-four.' Cat laughed with relief. Thinking of Holly, she felt she'd had a *very* lucky escape.

CHAPTER FOUR

Belle: Belgian Chocolates and True Confessions

'Shall we open those chocolates?' Belle asked as she settled down on the beanbags with Cat and Holly later that evening. 'They were on offer in Duty Free on the way over from New York and I couldn't resist them.'

'Hmm . . .' murmured Cat, pretending to think hard. 'Should we open the big box of Belgian chocolates or not? That's a difficult one! Oh, go on then, seeing as you're twisting my arm!'

'It'd be rude not to,' Holly agreed, grinning.

Cat reached over and started tearing off the cellophane.

Belle glanced happily around her room. It was smaller than she was used to, but bright and comfortable and prettily decorated in blues and turquoises. Her roommate, Cat, had already put up posters of glamorous 1950s movie stars like Marilyn Monroe and James Dean. And now Belle had her clothes hanging in the wardrobe, and her things arranged as she liked them.

It's all just perfect! she thought. *My first night at Superstar High! Sitting in my room chatting with new friends . . .*

They'd talked all through dinner already – but there was so much to talk *about*!

'We moved over to England from Dublin last year,' Cat was saying. 'My dad's a professor of ancient Irish history at Cambridge University. And my mum did a bit of film work years ago, so she was really keen for me to come here. I want to be a serious theatre actress, you know – the stage, the lights, the greasepaint. I can't believe I'm really here – at Superstar High!' She threw her hands in the air in celebration.

Holly smiled shyly. 'I'm just an ordinary girl from north London – my mum's a teacher and my stepdad's a gas-fitter,' she said. 'But I want to be a star! This is a dream come true for me!'

'Me too!' Belle agreed. 'I don't want much – just to be the greatest singer the world has ever seen!'

Holly and Cat both laughed. 'Whereabouts in America are you from?' Cat asked, unwrapping another chocolate.

Belle shrugged. 'Nowhere in particular. My parents

are both in show business and they're always travelling.' *Although not together*, she thought privately. Since her mom and dad separated when she was six, they had avoided even being in the same time zone. Belle had been shuffled between expensive apartments in New York and LA and luxury hotels in Europe. But she didn't want to talk about her celebrity parents. She hated to admit that her father was a famous film director and her mother a super-model. She didn't want anyone to think she was showing off.

'So I'm a bit of a nomad,' Belle continued. 'I don't have any siblings and I've always had private tutors and coaches – I've never even been to school before.'

'Wow!' Cat exclaimed. 'No school! How cool is that?'

'Not very!' Belle said wryly. 'It's just kind of *lonely*. I've never had any friends my own age.'

'That would be tough,' Holly said thoughtfully. 'I couldn't survive without my friends.'

'Yeah, me neither!' Cat agreed. 'Though the Garrick isn't like *normal* school. No uniform for a start. Whoever designed the uniform at my last school obviously didn't have red hair because it was pale grey and yellow! It made me look like the Corpse Bride . . .'

Belle sank back into her cushions, laughing. She was

having a such a great time! She was on the first rung of the magic ladder to singing stardom, *and* she had two amazing friends already! Cat was so funny and Holly was really sweet. Suddenly she felt the time was right to reveal her parents' identities – and get it over with. 'Er, I've got a confession to make . . .' she muttered.

'Ooh – you're a vampire?' Holly asked with a grin.

'Worse than that! It's my parents – they're—'

'Dirk Madison and Zoe Fairweather!' Cat finished for her matter-of-factly. 'I know! I overheard Bianca gossiping about it at dinner. She was telling everyone on her table what a "stuck-up cow" you are – and how her designer luggage wasn't good enough for you.'

A sick feeling churned in Belle's stomach. This was exactly what she had dreaded. Everyone would hate her before they even knew her! 'But I only said that thing about her luggage because she was being so mean to Holly,' she groaned. 'I'd never judge somebody by their luggage.'

'Phew!' Cat said. 'So I can bring my battered old cases out of hiding then.'

Holly threw a cushion at Cat. 'Don't worry, Belle. We're not going to let Bianca Hayford spoil Superstar High for us. Who cares what she says? We'll just rise above it!'

'R-i-i-i-s-e above it!' Cat echoed, standing on the bed and stretching out her arms like the wings of a soaring eagle.

'You're right.' Belle grinned, feeling her worries slip away, 'I am *so* rising above it!'

They were still chatting at nine o'clock, when Miss Candlemas, the housemistress, popped her head round the door, her broad frame swathed in bright printed fabrics and jangling with strings of beads. 'Hot chocolate delivery!' she announced, placing a tray on the coffee table. 'But don't expect room service every evening, gals! This is a first night only special! Own rooms by nine fifteen and lights out by ten please!'

Belle was asleep by 10.05!

CHAPTER FIVE

Cat: Mr Darcy and Star Quality

The next morning Cat heard Belle get out of bed. She forced open one eye and glimpsed her roommate slipping out of the door in co-ordinated pink running shorts and sports top. She glanced at her clock on the bedside table. It was 7 a.m. She *meant* to get up then too. She heard Belle come back in at 7.30. She *really, really* meant to get up then so that she'd have plenty of time to prepare for the tour of the school, which started at nine o'clock. In the end, of course, she leaped out of bed at 8.47, pulled on her trusty black mini-skirt and angora jumper and flew into the entrance hall, eye-liner in one hand, hairbrush in the other, with no breakfast and two minutes to spare.

Miss Candlemas was already handing out name-badges to the assembled students. 'Here,' Holly whispered, sneaking a piece of toast into Cat's hand. 'I was a bit late too. Do you want some of this?'

'Mm! Life-saver!' Cat mumbled through the

crumbs. *Holly's only known me a day and she can read my mind already!* she thought.

'Pop your name-badge on, dear,' Miss Candlemas chirped. 'Now, don't dilly-dally, people. Let's get this show on the road!'

'Move along now, campers,' a stocky, freckled boy with hair the colour of wet sand called out in a Scottish accent.

From the entrance hall 'at the heart of the original eighteenth-century building', they trooped into the dining room, with its ornately decorated ceiling and full-length windows. The serving area was tucked away at one end, and the long tables were covered in crisp white tablecloths. 'This was once the grand ballroom,' Miss Candlemas informed them.

Two ladies in hairnets and white aprons were tidying away after breakfast, but in Cat's imagination, Jane Austen heroines in ringlets and long dresses were dancing with handsome officers. Cat imagined herself there with them – she was Elizabeth Bennet in *Pride and Prejudice*. She had loved acting ever since she'd played Third Sheep in the school nativity play. Somehow she felt more real when she was in character than when she was being herself; even when she wasn't actually on stage, she was playing different roles in the virtual theatre in her head. 'Away with the fairies!' her dad called it.

Cat skipped a little step and held out her hand. 'Why, Mr Darcy, shall we dance?'

Oops, did I say that out loud? she wondered, hoping no one had noticed.

'How delightful to see you, Miss Bennet!'

Cat spun round to see who'd spoken. A skinny boy with wire-framed glasses and a floppy black fringe was grinning shyly back at her. She looked at his name-badge. It seemed that Nathan Almeida was a regular visitor to Fantasy World too! Cat smiled at him and winked – and then realized that the rest of the tour had moved on. She and Nathan grinned at each other and hurried after everyone else.

The tour snaked through the rest of the 'old school', taking in the common room, libraries, offices and function rooms, as well as the girls' accommodation upstairs. Then they followed Miss Candlemas through a door at the back of the hall into a pretty cobbled courtyard, making for the modern buildings arranged round the other three sides of the courtyard – through classrooms, state-of-the-art dance studios, recording studios and rehearsal rooms. 'Keep up!' Miss Candlemas called as she herded them round another shiny new block – this one housing the boys' rooms – and on to the sports centre.

'If you look to your right, campers, you'll see the Eiffel Tower,' the sandy-haired boy was saying, 'and to your left, the Taj Mahal . . .'

Cat peered across and read his name badge: NICK TAGGART.

Eventually they were ushered into the Redgrave, the school's purpose-built theatre. Cat loved all theatres, and the Redgrave was a beautiful one – she longed for the day when she could step out onto the elegant, curved stage and look out into a spellbound audience. The house lights were all on, illuminating the tiers of red plush seats. Cat breathed in the delicious theatre-smell of dust and nervous excitement, and sat down between Holly and Belle to watch the other new students file in for the welcome speeches.

Cat greeted Nathan Almeida with a friendly wave as he crept into the back row. Meanwhile Nick Taggart was goofing around with a bunch of other boys – Frankie Pellegrini, Zak Lomax and Mason Lee, according to their name-badges – pretending to be selling ice creams.

'Ice cream for you, miss?' Nick asked, plonking himself down in the seat next to Belle.

'Er, no, thank you,' Belle muttered politely.

'Ooh, go on,' Nick teased, imitating Belle's American accent and thrusting the imaginary tray of ice creams in her face. 'You know you want one! You're like totally drooooling for a Ben and Jerry's!'

'No, really I'm not!' Belle insisted, a little too loudly.

'Settle down, now!' warned one of the teachers, with a disapproving look at Belle and Nick.

'Uh-oh! Looks like we're on the Naughty Step already!' Nick grinned and tugged on one of Belle's long blonde plaits.

The boys all laughed, but Cat could see that Nick's in-your-face comedy routine was starting to freak Belle out. 'A white chocolate Magnum for me please,' she joked, to deflect his attention from her friend.

Belle looked relieved. 'What a dork!' she whispered.

Next, Bianca Hayford sashayed in, glancing around as if scanning for paparazzi. A serious-looking girl with wavy chestnut hair sat down next to her. 'That's Lettie Atkins,' Holly whispered. 'She called for Bianca this morning. They're friends from their old school.'

'*Lettie?*' Cat asked. 'Short for Lettuce?'

'Nicolette' – Holly grinned – 'but she said she got fed up with being called Knicker-ette. Some of the kids even called her Knickers!'

'Kids like Bianca probably! With friends like her, who'd need enemies?'

Everyone applauded as the principal strode onto the stage. James Fortune was still handsome – all crinkly blue eyes and white stubble – even though Cat thought he must be *ancient*. He'd been a famous actor-slash-heart-throb in the eighties. In fact, her mum had been downright *embarrassing* when they'd come for Cat's interview. She'd practically swooned when Mr Fortune arrived. She'd even started going on about how she'd been in a *Star Wars* movie.

'Oh, what part?' Mr Fortune had asked her, looking a little baffled. Cat's mum was only four feet some-thing, which obviously placed certain limits on the roles she could play.

'We filmed in California, of course . . .' Mum had muttered in response, suddenly keen to change the subject.

Mr Fortune had looked puzzled.

'Mum was an Ewok,' Cat had put in quietly, noticing the principal's stifled grin.

Her mother had glared at her. 'Of course, *some* people think the Ewoks were just glorified teddy bears!' she'd told him defensively. 'But there was a lot more to it than that, I'll have you know!'

Cat prayed silently that Mr Fortune had blanked the entire episode from his mind.

'Welcome to the Garrick School!' He took a moment to adjust the microphone. 'We study a balanced curriculum. Academic subjects in the mornings' – there was a groan from the audience at the word *academic* – 'and performing arts in the afternoons . . .' There was a loud cheer. 'As well as core lessons in singing, dancing and acting,' he continued, pacing up and down, hands clasped behind his back, 'each student has been enrolled in *advanced* classes according to their individual abilities. However' – he paused for dramatic effect – 'over the next few weeks, teachers will be observing lessons to identify students whose hidden talents we may have missed. If you work hard, you may be invited to join *additional* advanced classes after half-term.'

Cat felt her heart race. Although acting was her Big Thing, and she'd already been selected for advanced acting classes, she'd love to earn a place in advanced Latin American dance too!

'Finally' – Mr Fortune beamed – 'as you all know, the Garrick School is nicknamed Superstar High. But being a star is about more that just sparkling on the outside. True superstars shine on the *inside* too. You've all proved you have star potential. Our mission now is to help you develop into well-rounded people – who also happen to be performing arts professionals with that all-important *star quality*!'

CHAPTER SIX

Cat: First Impressions

It was Wednesday afternoon. Cat was on her way to the first dance class of term, trailing behind Holly and Belle. 'I wish we were starting with Latin dance,' she grumbled. 'I love salsa and cha-cha-cha! Anything with a bit of passion!' She paused to stomp out a series of flamboyant flamenco steps.

'Sorry, but the timetable clearly says, *Girls – ballet – all levels – Miss Morgan*,' Belle told her.

'Miss Morgan was a judge at the Steps to the Stars competition,' Holly added. 'She's great but she's really fierce!'

'Just what I need.' Cat grimaced. 'I did ballet when I was a kid, but I wasn't much good. I just don't like it really.'

'I love it,' Holly said. 'It's got everything – strength . . . grace . . . control . . .'

Miss Drusilla Morgan, head of the Dance Department, was waiting for them in the dance studio – a tiny wizened gnome of a woman in an old-fashioned black leotard, her white hair pulled back in a bun under a wide elastic hairband.

'Off with them!' she screeched, banging her stick on the floor as the girls stepped out from the changing room. 'No hiding under those dreadful T-shirts! I want a good look at you all today, before I split you up into ability groups – advanced, intermediate and . . .'

Complete no-hopers, Cat thought as she pulled her baggy black T-shirt over her head. She felt *way* out of her comfort-zone in her new navy leotard. She'd never felt particularly boob-heavy before, but now she was surrounded by girls the size of toothbrushes. She suddenly felt like a Yorkshire pudding in a pancake house.

'Hair up!' Miss Morgan yelled.

Cat had tethered her hair into a loose knot, but this obviously wasn't 'up' enough. Miss Morgan snatched a handful of curls and scraped them back, anchoring them to Cat's head with sharp little hair-grips which she plucked from her own hairband.

This must be what it feels like to have a face-lift, Cat thought.

As they started the barre exercises, Cat couldn't help comparing herself to the other girls as she worked through her *pliés* and *tendus*. She hated to admit it, but

Bianca Hayford was very good. Belle was all elegance and poise, of course. Gemma Dalrymple, a tall bronzed athletic-looking Australian girl, and Serena Quereshi, a petite Pakistani girl from Manchester, were also excellent ballerinas. But it was Holly who really stood out! Especially when they moved on to the faster *allegro* section; she was as graceful as a butterfly.

'*Magnifica*, Holly. *Che bellezza!*' Miss Morgan cried, clapping her hands as Holly executed another perfect *grand jeté*.

Cat wasn't entirely sure *why* her exclamations were in Italian. As far as she could tell, Drusilla Morgan was no more Italian than a tin of spaghetti hoops. But, whatever the reason, Cat definitely didn't bring out the Italian in her.

'Pull up! Bottom in! Shoulders down!' Miss Morgan told her as Cat took up her position on the back row for the *enchaînements*. 'You are not without talent, Catrin, but you must work! I want to see sweat!'

If I sweat any more I'll dissolve, Cat thought, exchanging a pained grin with Belle.

Cat remembered Holly's words — *strength, grace, control. That just about sums up everything I'm not!* she thought. She decided she'd just have to *act* the part of a dancer! She'd be Darcey Bussell in *Swan Lake*. No, she would be Holly! She imagined her body losing its curves, and her muscles becoming toned and lithe . . .

'That's much better, Catrin!' Miss Morgan shouted, smiling at her for the first time.

It was all going so well. She could be a butterfly too!

'*Bene!* Catrin' – Miss Morgan beamed – 'come to the front row! Now, tell me, what are the key qualities in a ballerina?'

Cat grinned. 'Ooh, I know this. *Strength, grace, control . . .*' she said.

There was a long silence. She looked up. Everyone was staring at her. What had she said? OK, she wasn't exactly the Einstein of the ballet world, but they were Holly's words and she was fairly sure Holly knew her stuff.

Next to her, Belle was desperately trying to communicate something with her eyebrows. Then Cat realized it wasn't *what* she'd said, it was the *way* she'd said it. She'd plunged so far into character that she'd accidentally answered in Holly's north London accent.

'Instead of *mocking* those with more talent than yourself, Catrin,' Miss Morgan shouted, banging her stick, 'you would do better to try and *learn* something from them.'

'I wasn't mock—' Cat started, but Miss Morgan had already moved on to the next sequence.

Behind her, she heard Bianca barely suppressing her sniggers. Suddenly she felt more like a big hairy caterpillar than a butterfly!

Thank the Lord the lesson isn't mixed, she thought; at least none of the boys were there to witness her public humiliation.

Cat glanced towards Holly at the end of the row, hoping her new friend hadn't been offended. Holly's shoulders were trembling. *Oh, no – she wasn't crying, was she?* Cat spent the rest of the lesson trying to catch Holly's eye. Finally they passed in a rapid *glissade* sequence across the studio. 'Sorry, I didn't mean to—' Cat mouthed.

'I know!' Holly whispered back, fighting to keep her composure as a snort of giggles escaped her.

'*Silenzio!*' screeched Miss Morgan. 'Ballet class is no place for idle chit-chat!'

'That went well then!' Cat sighed, grinning ruefully at Holly and Belle as they changed out of their dance clothes at the end of the class. 'It's so-o-o important to make a good first impression on the teachers, I always think!'

CHAPTER SEVEN

Holly: Butterflies and Cinderella

The only butterflies Holly felt as she entered Mr Grampian's acting class the next afternoon were the ones fluttering around in her stomach. Acting was her weakest link. She could get up on stage and dance any time. And singing was no problem either. But when it came to straight acting, she felt like a fish out of water. It was as if she were lost without a soundtrack. But she was determined to conquer her doubts and improve – she knew that to succeed in the competitive world of musical theatre she would need all three strings to her bow.

Leslie Grampian – or Hawk-man, as Holly thought of him – had a mane of flowing white hair and an alarmingly hooked beak-like nose. He also had a strange just-swallowed-the-dictionary style of speaking that meant that she wasn't always *entirely* sure what he was talking about. All of which just added to her anxiety. So when he asked them to get into groups of three and enact their own version of a 'five-minute fairy tale', Holly's butterflies went into overdrive.

'Ten minutes' brainstorming to formulate your scenario!' Mr Grampian called out.

'What's up, Hols?' Cat asked. 'You look as if you're about to be sick!'

'Just a bit nervous . . .' Holly muttered.

'OK then, you be Cinderella,' Belle said briskly. 'Nervous will be *perfect* for that part. Cat and I will be the Ugly Sisters. Cat, you be loud and I'll be—'

'Very, very bossy?' Cat suggested with a grin.

Belle's eyebrows quivered uncertainly.

'Cat was just kidding!' Holly explained. She'd noticed that in spite of her style and sophistication, Belle hadn't quite got to grips with some of the more basic everyday concepts of friendship – like *teasing*, for example. It was probably something to do with not having been to school; after all, being teased was one of the first lessons you learned there – along with tying your shoelaces and putting your hand up to go to the loo.

'Sorry, I'll wave a flag next time,' said Cat. 'Oh, and that was more kidding!' she added, holding her hands up in surrender.

Belle grinned and looked relieved.

Cat turned to Holly. 'Come on, then, Cinders. Let's get to work.'

'So, here's what we should do—' Belle began.

'Ooh, Belle thinks she's a big-shot director, *just like Daddy*!' Holly heard Bianca say loudly to her group. Cat and Belle had not missed the snide comment either.

'*R-i-i-i-sing* . . .' Holly started to whisper, and the other two joined in with a chorus of, '*R-i-i-i-sing above it!*' Cat added a discreet aeroplane-taking-off gesture with one hand.

'As I was saying . . .' Belle continued with a smile.

When it was their turn to perform to the class, Holly took her position and concentrated on sweeping ashes from a make-believe fire. When Belle marched into the imaginary kitchen and ordered her to iron her new Christian Lacroix dress, she jumped up and stammered her apologies for not having done it earlier. Then Cat flounced in, hair speedily back-combed into a bird's-nest tangle, a giant wart crafted from Blu-Tack in the middle of her nose. 'Cinders, what have you done with my goat-urine-and-thistle beauty cream?' she screamed, so loudly that Holly actually jumped, even though she knew that was what Cat was going to say.

'I haven't touched it!' Holly trembled. Ugly Sister

Cat took a sly glance at Holly's pretty face, then reached out a hand, as if unable to resist touching the soft skin. Then she ran her fingers over her own face. The class was silent as they watched the Ugly Sister sadly comparing her own grotesque complexion with Cinderella's natural beauty. Then they laughed again as Cat 'accidentally' kicked over the dustpan and told Holly to sweep it all up again.

Holly grinned with relief as the class applauded and Mr Grampian beamed. 'Excellent! Superlative characterization, all of you!'

But he singled Cat out for special praise. 'Splendid! That hint of poignant sadness in the middle of the comic performance was inspired!'

He's right, Holly thought. *Cat really is a brilliant actress.*

'Isn't Mr Grampian just the loveliest teacher in the entire Solar System?' Cat enthused as they left the class a little later.

'Maybe,' Holly said. She didn't feel *quite* as terrified of Hawk-man as she had at the start of the class, but she wasn't sure she'd stretch to *lovely*! She'd rather have Miss Morgan any day. 'Thanks for helping me out back there,' she added.

'You did fine, Hols.' Cat smiled and gave her a hug.

'You'll be winning Oscars before you know it!' Belle added.

'No, I think that'll be Cat's job.'

As they entered the main corridor, Holly paused to read a poster on the Drama Department notice board. 'Hey, Cat,' she said, 'you have got to try for this!'

Cat studied the poster: beneath a blood-soaked dagger were the words, MACBETH AUDITIONS NOW OPEN: YEARS 8–10.

'Yes, Catrin, your friend is indubitably correct. That would be a most auspicious decision!' Mr Grampian announced as he strode past, balancing an enormous tray of coffees.

Holly and Cat exchanged puzzled looks. 'Erm, *auspicious . . .*' Cat murmured. 'Does that mean it would be a good idea or a bad idea?'

Belle laughed. 'It means *You go for it, girl.*'

CHAPTER EIGHT

Cat: Algebra and Other Problems

It wasn't until Friday evening that Cat had a moment to herself. She snuggled down on her bed, laptop on her knee, to write an e-mail to her sister. *This place is amazing!* she typed. *It's like Disneyland and High School Musical rolled into one!*

Cat had never actually been to Disneyland. But neither had her eight-year-old sister, Fiona, so she allowed herself a little artistic licence. They'd both seen all the *High School Musical* films, of course – again and again.

My roommate is called Belle, Cat continued. *She's American and she wants to be a famous singer. And my other best friend, Holly, is a brilliant dancer* . . .

Cat stretched. Since Wednesday's ballet class she had felt as if she'd been in the scrum for the Irish rugby team. She stroked Shreddie, who – with blatant disregard for school rules – was curled up on her bed, kneading her maths book with his velvet paws. Which reminded Cat – she was *meant* to be doing homework. It was so unfair! The Garrick was a stage school – why did they have to study all these boring school subjects? It was Super*star* High, wasn't it? Not Super*nerd* High!

English was OK, but maths and science gave her brain pins and needles. Cat prised the book from Shreddie's claws and frowned at the algebra symbols. *She was Hermione Granger poring over a book of spells in Hogwarts' library: 'If X is equal to two Y squared . . .'* she chanted in an ultra-brainy voice, waving her pencil in the air like a wand.

It didn't help.

Cat sighed and gazed around the room. Her eyes lingered on the jumble of family photographs she'd pinned on her corkboard. A warm evening breeze ruffled the curtains at the open window. Voices drifted up from the courtyard far below. Someone somewhere was practising the violin.

Belle and Holly had gone off to the sports centre for a swim.

So here she was.

In her room.

By herself.

All alone.

Cat had thought it would be great fun living at

the Garrick, away from her batty mum, her dad – who was more at home in twelfth-century Ireland than twenty-first-century Cambridge – her noisy twin brothers and even Fiona. She adored her sister, but she could be hard work at times. And it *was* fun. She loved it. But she'd had no idea she'd miss her family so much!

The lump in Cat's throat suddenly bull-frogged into a sob.

And then another.

Belle and Holly would be back soon, she realized. She couldn't let them see her like this. *She was good old Cat – the life and soul of the party!*

Chin up, old bean! Let's have none of this blubbing, she chided herself in her best *Malory Towers* voice. But it was no use. She was *seriously* homesick. And now an image popped into her head of her little dog, Duffy, sitting waiting at the back door for her to come in from school.

Tears flowed down her cheeks and dropped onto Shreddie's fur. She loved life at Superstar High. But she *really* wanted to go home – just for a visit. If she left now, she could get a train and be there in a couple of hours . . .

CHAPTER NINE

Belle: Chlorine and Karaoke

At that moment Belle was climbing out of the swimming pool.

'Wow! That's what I call *class*!' came a boy's voice from the top of the steps.

Belle looked up to see a drop-dead-gorgeous boy with short dark hair and green eyes, chatting to the lifeguard.

She smiled, pleased at the compliment. It was the first time she'd worn her new white Versace bikini and she hadn't been sure it suited her.

'Smooth leg action,' the boy continued, 'nice strong arms . . .'

Hel-lo! Getting way too personal here! Belle thought.

'She breathes really well too,' the lifeguard agreed.

Belle had never considered breathing to be a particular skill – except in singing class, of course . . . That's when she realized they weren't even looking at her. They were watching Holly slicing through the water like a miniature torpedo in Speedo goggles.

Belle sighed as she blow-dried her hair in the changing room. Holly really was a good swimmer. And a great dancer too. And Cat was so lively and fun and such a talented actress. And their families sounded so nice and *normal*. She couldn't help feeling just a little bit jealous . . .

Wouldn't it be great to be noticed for something other than your designer clothes and your famous parents? she thought to herself.

Ever since she could remember, all Belle had wanted was to be a singer. And if there was anywhere that dream could come true, then it was here at Superstar High! Belle loved everything about the Garrick. OK, *almost* everything. Having to share a bathroom was proving a little hard to get used to. And then there was Bianca, of course . . .

One day, Belle thought, grinning at her reflection as the smell of scorched hair snapped her out of her reverie and made her turn off the hairdryer, *one day, people will look at me and they won't say, 'Isn't she Dirk Madison's daughter?' or 'Hey, her mom's Zoe Fairweather!' They'll say, 'Wow, that's Belle Madison, international singing superstar — La Diva!'*

Returning to her room, Belle put her bottle of

water and her purse down on the coffee table. Holly followed her in, and knocked them off with her swimming bag as she dived onto a beanbag, scattering drops of pool water from her soggy braids.

'I think I'll stick to yoga in future,' Belle said, hanging her towel neatly on the radiator.

Cat was sitting on her bed, wearing a satin bathrobe over a sparkly mini-dress. Her laptop was lying open next to her.

What's wrong with this picture? Belle wondered.

Cat was silent. Cat wasn't laughing . . . but Cat was always laughing!

Holly must have noticed it too. 'Hey, Cat?' she asked gently. 'Have you been crying?'

Cat swallowed hard and cracked a grin. 'Oh, no, of course not! It's just that I, erm . . . er . . . poked myself in the eye with my wand – erm, I mean *pencil*—'

'With your *wand*?' Belle asked incredulously.

But Cat was already acting out an over-the-top pantomime of stabbing herself in the eye – much to Shreddie's irritation. He jumped down from the bed and padded out of the room.

That wouldn't make both *eyes red, would it?* Belle thought. She followed Holly's glance towards the floor – a small holdall was spilling out its contents of underwear and make-up. 'Are you going somewh—?' Belle started to ask, but Holly stopped her with a don't-go-there kind of look. Then Belle noticed the family photograph that Cat was stuffing under her pillow. *Poor Cat! She must be homesick!* Belle realized. She'd never experienced homesickness but she could see that her friend was really suffering.

'Well, I know those algebra problems really suck, but blinding yourself to get out of doing them seems a little *drastic*!' Holly teased.

Belle was surprised for a moment that Holly – who was always so kind – was making a joke when Cat was clearly upset. But then she saw that it had worked perfectly. Cat grinned and started to look like her old self again.

'Yeah, come to the library with me before breakfast tomorrow and we'll work on them together,' Belle added, following Holly's lead and sitting down on the bed next to Cat.

Cat smiled gratefully. 'What is this *be-fore break-fast* of which you speak?' she asked, pretending to be puzzled. 'Unknown concept – cannot compute!'

Soon they were all rolling on the bed laughing; Belle could almost *see* her old vocal coach, Daphne, shaking her head in horror, 'All that cackling – you'll damage your larynx!' Daphne would have said. But, for now, Belle was prepared to live dangerously. Sometimes friends were more important than vocal cords.

'Right, I'm off to my room to get changed,' Holly announced a little while later. As she opened the door to leave, Belle heard a commotion in the corridor.

'That creature's lurking outside my room *again*!' Bianca yelled. 'Lettie, get rid of it!'

Belle peeped out of the door and smiled when she saw Shreddie curled up outside Bianca and Holly's room. Shreddie liked Cat because she allowed him on her bed. But for some unfathomable feline reason, he absolutely *adored* Bianca Hayford.

'Oh, look,' Bianca snorted, pointing at Belle and Holly, and then holding her nose. 'It's the Chlorine Doreens! They must have found a *puddle* to swim in! Or maybe Daddy's bought little Belle her own pool! Euurghh! The chlorine fumes are making me sick! Come on, Lettie, we need to start getting ready!'

Rise above it, Belle told herself. *Rise above it!*

Lettie giggled awkwardly, then picked Shreddie up and handed him to Holly, before following Bianca into her room.

'Get ready for what?' Holly murmured, hovering in the doorway.

'Personality of the Year awards?' Cat suggested from behind her.

'*Rise above it!*' Belle reminded her.

'Of course! It's the party! Tonight in the common room!' Cat exclaimed. 'I can't believe we forgot about it!' She ushered Holly back into the room, slamming the door shut behind her.

Belle felt a sudden tingle of anticipation – she'd attended hundreds of film premieres, fashion shows and receptions, but she'd never been to a school party before. She couldn't wait!

'I'm not really dressed for a party' – Holly hesitated – 'and I can't go back to my room and change now. Bianca'll start going on about the chlorine again. She calls it "chemical warfare"!'

Holly's so petite and pretty that she always looks great, Belle thought. But she could see that the damp-tracksuit-and-slipper-socks combo was probably not her *best* look. 'No problem!' She handed Holly a pink Abercrombie & Fitch T-shirt and some cropped jeans from her wardrobe. 'Try these!'

'And the best thing is,' Cat added, 'they've got a karaoke machine!'

'*Auspicious!*' Holly grinned as she pulled on the clothes. The jeans were full-length on her, and slipping off her hips.

'Here, use this . . .' Belle gave her a leather belt with a big silver buckle.

'And these would look great on you!' Cat added, throwing Holly a pair of chunky silver bangles.

Belle picked out her favourite jeans and a simple white Stella McCartney top for herself. Then she smoothed her hair with straightening irons. Meanwhile Cat was accessorizing her black mini-dress with black tights and zebra-print stilettos. Belle pretended not to notice as she retrieved her make-up bag from the half-packed holdall, before kicking it out of sight under the bed.

'Well, what are we waiting for?' Cat cried, gathering her hair into a messy up-do and applying a final slick of lip gloss. 'It's Friday night! Let's *par*-tay!' She threw her arms around Belle and Holly and conga-danced them out of the door. 'Forget Girls Aloud! Never mind The Sugababes! Make way for the Chlorine Doreens!'

Holly laughed. 'That must be the worst name for a girl band I've ever heard!'

And this, Belle thought, *is the best Friday night I've ever had. And the party hasn't even started yet!*

* ★ ★

The end-of-first-week party was a Garrick tradition. The older students organized it every year to welcome the new intake. They'd transformed the common room with disco lights and mirror balls and provided food and drinks. Belle helped herself to a mineral water while Cat grabbed a Fanta and a handful of peanuts. Holly was already on the dance floor.

Belle wasn't surprised to see Nick Taggart and his friends already up at the karaoke machine, belting out *Bohemian Rhapsody*. She cringed as Nick winked at her a few minutes later. 'This is for our American *belle* of the ball!' he shouted, launching into Bruce Springsteen's *Born in the USA*.

'Not sure about this music!' Holly grimaced, tripping over Belle's foot as she stepped off the dance floor and helped herself to Cat's Fanta.

'Come on, we've got to do *something* to stop these guys hogging the karaoke all night.' Cat pulled Holly and Belle along with her. 'Belle, you choose!'

Belle studied the song choices on the screen of the karaoke machine. She'd never sung with Cat and Holly before, so she picked something everyone would know. Abba was always a good bet.

She needn't have worried. The girls complemented

each other perfectly. Cat's voice was husky and powerful, while Holly had the sweet tone of a choir girl. They absolutely nailed *Dancing Queen*. Belle saw all the students flood onto the dance floor – except for Nathan Almeida and Lettie Atkins, who watched quietly from the back.

There was wild applause, then shouts for more. 'OK!' Cat laughed as they launched into an energetic version of *It's Raining Men*.

As the music faded out, Bianca Hayford marched up to the karaoke machine.

Holly smiled and handed her the microphone. 'Here, Bianca, you have a go!'

'About time too!' Bianca snapped.

As Bianca started singing *My Heart Will Go On*, Belle listened in stunned silence. *Wow! Bianca can* really *sing!* she thought. *How can such a bitter person have such a sweet voice?*

Belle was listening so intently that it was a moment before she tuned in to the mumble of discontent around her. The students were all standing around the edges of the empty dance floor.

'Her heart's going on . . . and on . . . and on . . .' Zak muttered to Frankie, Mason and Nick.

Belle turned to look at the boys standing behind

her. 'What's the problem?' she asked. 'Bianca has an *awesome* voice . . .'

'It's a time-and-a-place thing!' Frankie explained. 'It's *way* too early for a slow ballad!'

'Yeah, we're *Stokaboka*, man!' Zak wailed. 'We've got our dancing pants on!'

Belle glanced down. Zak was wearing a pair of baggy Bermuda shorts. With his long sun-streaked hair and deep tan, Zak Lomax looked – and sounded – like a surf-dude waiting for the next big wave.

'Yeah, come on, girls. Let's get this party back on track.' Nick flung his arms round Belle, Cat and Holly and marched them towards the karaoke machine.

Belle protested – but she had to admit, if only to herself, that in fact she was *dying* to get back to the karaoke machine with Holly and Cat. This time they sang *Girls Just Wanna Have Fun*. Belle watched in delight as the dance floor filled up again and Nick gave her a big thumbs-up sign.

Was he laughing at her? Belle wondered. It was hard to tell. But one thing was for sure: he really was a bit of a dork!

When the track ended, Belle high-fived triumphantly with her two friends.

Cat laughed. 'Wow! That was fun!'

'Brilliant!' Holly agreed.

Their eyes were sparkling with exhilaration; Belle couldn't remember ever feeling this alive! Singing with Holly and Cat was amazing! It was as if someone had just turned the volume control on her life up to maximum.

'Awesome!' she gasped through the grip of Cat's bear hug. So awesome, in fact, that it had given her a truly *awesome* idea . . .

CHAPTER TEN

Belle: Harmony and the Class Clown

Over the weekend Belle was so busy, she decided she'd better keep her truly awesome idea to herself. At least for now.

They'd already been given piles of homework, and she stayed up late on Sunday night finishing a science report on electrical circuits.

Now it was Monday afternoon and Mr Garcia's singing class was drawing to a close. They'd been working on vocal harmony. Belle had enjoyed the lesson, but as they sat in a circle in the warm studio, with the rain drumming rhythmically on the windows, she started to feel v-e-r-y, v-e-r-y s-l-e-e-p-y . . .

'So you'll need to work with a partner for this assignment . . .' Mr Garcia's deep voice rumbled.

Belle shook herself and sat up straight. *Where am I? Assignment? What assignment?*

'Belle, will you be my partner?' Nick Taggart had thrown himself at her feet, landing on bended knee as if proposing marriage. 'Say you will or my heart will break in two!' he begged.

'Fabulous idea!' Mr Garcia boomed, rubbing his gleaming bald mahogany-brown head as if to polish it further. 'Nick and Belle, you should be able to come up with something really interesting!'

'Oh, yeah, *really* interesting!' Bianca Hayford muttered.

'I'm a little shaky on the details of this assignment,' Belle whispered to Holly and Cat as they stacked away the chairs. She was *not* going to admit, even to her closest friends, that she'd fallen asleep in class.

Holly grinned. 'Yeah, I noticed you were *resting your eyes* for a moment there! Each pair has to pick a pop or rock song – then work out two-part harmonies and record them on a CD . . .'

'*By next week!*' Cat mouthed, her grey eyes wide with indignation.

'Howdy, pardner,' Nick drawled in an American accent, catching up with Belle as they left the studio. 'Let's mosey on down to the ole music library and pick ourselves out one helluva song.'

Belle nodded reluctantly, grimacing at Nick's Texan cowboy impression. In fact, she thought as she followed him to the music library, Nick's natural lilting Scottish accent was pretty much the only thing about him she liked. Belle took her singing very seriously, and she was quite sure that Nick did not. He was a loud-mouth and a show-off who spent all his time doing dumb voices and acting the class clown. And now she was stuck with him for an entire week.

'After you, ma'am!' Nick steered Belle through the door of the music library, where floor-to-ceiling shelves were crammed with CDs and musical scores. Several students were sitting at the computer stations in the centre of the room. Others were browsing along the shelves or listening to music through headphones in booths arranged along one side. Settling down at a free computer, Nick raked back his hair – so thick and straw-like, it reminded Belle of the thatched roofs of cottages she'd seen when she'd visited the English countryside – then jabbed expertly at the keyboard and pulled the library catalogue up on the screen. 'What'll it be, m'lady? Metallica? Kiss? Ice-T?'

An hour later Belle found Holly in the common room, eating toast and Marmite and chatting about ballet with a group of Year Ten girls, including Lucy Cheng. The common room, now restored to normal operation after the karaoke party, was furnished with big squashy easy chairs. There was a widescreen TV at one end and a kitchen area at the other. There was even a huge open fire for winter. The walls were covered with signed photographs of old Garrick students – who were now international superstars.

Belle joined Holly and started to fix herself a peanut butter and jelly sandwich. The older girls drifted off to the other end of the common room to watch TV.

'So, did you and Nick find a "helluva" song?' Holly asked her.

'No way! He's into all kinds of wacko heavy metal stuff. I just don't get it! Why was he so keen to work with me?'

'Duh!' Holly laughed. 'Maybe it's the fact that you're the best singer in the class *by miles*. And, oh yeah, perhaps because he fancies you!'

'*Fancies* me?' Belle asked.

'You know, has a crush on you . . . wants to go out with you . . . ?'

'I know what it means! But Nick Taggart? He's such a . . . clown!'

'Well, clowns have feelings too,' Holly replied.

'Anyway' – Belle frowned – 'Bianca is just as good a singer as I am. Why didn't he want to work with her?'

'Hel–lo!' Holly said, giggling. 'Nick may be a clown but he's not completely *insane*!'

'Oh, look, here's Cat.' Belle changed the subject from the deeply unpleasant notion of Nick Taggart *fancying* her. Her idea of the perfect guy was a tall dark handsome Johnny Depp look–alike: cool, sophisticated – and with a singing voice to die for, of course. Nick Taggart most certainly did not fit the bill!

Cat was with Nathan Almeida. They were both carrying piles of books and laughing, but Nathan stopped short when he saw the other girls and immediately started sidling towards the door. Belle smiled; Nathan was from Mexico, but he was a million miles away from her carnival–and–fiesta–party–animal image of a Latin American guy. To say that Nathan was *shy* would be like saying that Mariah Carey was an *OK* singer. The only person who'd broken through his shell was Cat.

'Nathan's going to help me with my electric circuits!' Cat said, helping herself to toast. 'Mrs Salmon threatened me with a detention or instant death or something if I don't hand that report in tomorrow!'

'And I'm sure The Fish won't let you off the hook!' Holly joked.

Those circuits have a lot to answer for, Belle thought.

If she'd not stayed up working on them until midnight she wouldn't have fallen asleep in the singing class and could have escaped being paired with Nick on the harmony assignment!

'We're off to the study room!' Cat waved as she shimmied out of the room, Nathan hot on her heels.

'He's supposed to be a very gifted actor,' Belle whispered, 'but I've never even heard him speak, let alone act.'

'Maybe he's a mime artist?' Holly said, performing a brief attempting-to-escape-from-a-glass-box mime.

Belle grinned. 'Boys! Are they *all* weird or is it just the ones *we* know?'

CHAPTER ELEVEN

Holly: Pirouettes and the Kiss of Life

Later on Monday afternoon Holly was leaving her room with her dance bag over her shoulder. She'd booked one of the small studios to practise her *pirouettes* with some of the other keen ballerinas. Miss Morgan had made it clear that all dancers should be putting in several hours' practice a week outside of lesson time, especially the 'elite' group, and Holly was determined to live up to expectations.

Holly had invited Belle and Cat to come along, of course, but Belle was busy working on her maths homework and Cat had also declined. In fact, her exact words were: 'I'd rather flush my head down the toilet . . .' Ballet was not flavour of the month with Cat!

Suddenly Bianca appeared in the corridor with Lettie and Mayu Tanaka. Mayu was Bianca's new best friend. With dark almond-shaped eyes and long black hair in ribbon-tied bunches, she looked as cute as one of those little Japanese Kimmi Dolls. But she had a lot in common with Bianca – a mean streak as wide as the M25, for one thing.

Holly's first instinct was to hide, but she forced herself to stand her ground. She'd seen bullies in action at her old school, and from the moment she'd realized she was sharing a room with one she'd made a conscious decision not to be intimidated. She deployed the Shield of Full-on Friendliness as her main defence.

'Anyone like to join me for some ballet practice?' she asked.

Lettie put down her cello case and looked as if she was about to accept. Although Lettie's speciality was music, Holly had noticed that she was also an excellent dancer. But Bianca spoke for all of them: 'Er, I don't *think* so!'

'Like we even need the extra practice!' Mayu sneered in her little-girl voice that should have been sweet but somehow always managed to sound bitchy.

'Yeah!' Lettie mumbled rather unconvincingly.

'OK, but if you change your mind, Lettie, I'll be in studio seven,' Holly called over her shoulder as she hurried off down the corridor.

Some time later, Holly glanced at the clock and nearly jumped out of her skin – which would have been tricky, as she was standing on one leg with the other foot tucked in behind her knee.

It was twenty-five past seven! Everyone else had left, but Holly was still in the dance studio. After almost two hours she was snapping her *pirouettes* round so fast that she was in danger of getting whiplash. Something magical always happened when she was dancing: she shook off the clumsy-klutz Holly of the everyday world and shifted into a completely different dimension.

And she always lost track of time.

Holly gazed into the mirror-wall behind the barre. It was not a pretty sight: face shining with sweat, her hairband fighting a losing battle with her braids. And people thought that ballet was such a ladylike pursuit!

If you don't get to the dining hall in the next five minutes, you'll miss dinner, she told her reflection.

And Monday was pizza-and-salad-bar night. Her favourite!

Figuring that a rush to the dining room would be as good as a warm-down, she tore off her ballet shoes, pulled on sweat pants and stuffed her feet into trainers. It was now 7.26. She helter-skeltered down the stairs, elbowing her way through a group of students and instrument cases. Taking the last five steps in a single bound, Holly propelled herself through the double doors into the courtyard. She banked sharply round the corner and sprinted towards the back door of the entrance hall.

Suddenly she was burying her head in a football shirt.

She was flying backwards through the air.

She was landing on the path on her derrière.

Holly cracked open one eye and saw a flurry of pages drifting down around her, followed by a muddy football, which landed – *smack* – in the middle of her forehead.

Ow! That really hurt! Holly thought, but she was too winded even to groan.

'Great block tackle!' a boy's voice was saying somewhere. 'We could do with her in our back four!'

'Yeah, she'd do better than you!' someone laughed, as if from a great distance.

Holly struggled to sit up and focus on a face that was now only inches away. Short dark hair. Sea-green eyes. Square jaw. Hang on, she recognized that jaw. It was the one that had once worn the Victorian beard. It belonged to Ethan Reed. She'd noticed him at the swimming pool a few times too. Not just *noticed* him, in fact, but really *noticed* him . . .

He was absolutely stop-whatever-you're-doing-and-stare-till-your-eyes-pop-out gorgeous.

And, she'd heard – Ethan Reed being the kind of person people talked about *a lot* – that not only was he a brilliant actor; he was also a freestyle swimming champion *and* captain of the school football team – which explained the ball.

'Are you OK?' he asked.

And now he was gently touching her neck. *He must be feeling for a pulse*, Holly thought. *Oh, no! He'll try the kiss of life next if I'm not careful!*

'Don't kiss me, I'm alive!' she squeaked.

Ethan laughed. 'Yeah, I usually only kiss dead girls!' he said.

Oh, brilliant! Holly berated herself. *Congratulations, Miss Holly Devenish, Idiot of the Year.* Not content with head-butting Ethan Reed in the chest, she had now addressed him with the single most stupid sentence ever to be uttered in the entire history of mankind: *Don't kiss me, I'm alive.*

If she lived to be a hundred, she knew that sentence would haunt her for the rest of her life.

'I'm really sorry,' Ethan was saying, putting his arm around her shoulders to help her up. 'I didn't see you flying round the corner at the speed of light. I didn't *mean* to bombard you with footballs . . .'

'I only had four minutes—' Holly stopped. She was babbling again.

'Hey, I remember you!' Ethan said. 'It's Holly, isn't it? We carried your bags upstairs on the first day of term.'

'Yes, that's right,' Holly mumbled. 'With your beard . . .' *Argh!* she screamed to herself. When exactly had she lost the ability to speak normally?

There was a pause while Ethan processed the *beard* part. 'Right!' He laughed. 'The Victorian costumes! We'd been doing a film shoot; a Christmas Special for CBBC.'

'Oh yeah!' said the other boy, who Holly now realized was Felix Baddeley. 'What on earth did you have in that backpack by the way? I was soaking by the time we got to your room.'

Could this encounter get any more humiliating? Holly wondered.

It could. And it did.

'And I've seen you in the pool too,' Ethan said. 'I didn't recognize you with your clothes on for a minute.'

Felix guffawed and Ethan paused, embarrassed. 'Sorry,' he said with a sheepish grin. 'That didn't come out right! I haven't seen you with *no* clothes on – obviously. I don't hang around spying through the keyholes in the girls' changing room or anything like that. I meant, I've seen you in your swimming costume – I love your breathing—'

Am I hearing this right? Holly wondered. *Is Ethan really talking complete and utter gibberish – just like me? That's so sweet!*

'Er, guys,' Felix interrupted. 'I hate to break up the party, but we need to get to the gym. Circuit training, remember?'

'And I've got to get to dinner,' Holly mumbled.

'You'll have missed it now,' Ethan said, pulling her to her feet. 'Here, take this,' he added, tugging a yellow-napkin-wrapped item from his pocket. 'Piece of pepperoni and anchovy pizza. I was saving it for later.'

'Oh, no, I couldn't,' Holly gasped, eyeing the greasy wedge of paper suspiciously.

'I insist!'

Very gingerly, Holly took the pizza and started heading towards the double doors into the hall.

'Hope I bump into you again soon!' Ethan called after her.

Holly opened the first door she came to. And

walked into a rack of cabbages. This wasn't the hall! She was in some kind of storeroom. After a few moments among the vegetables she stumbled across a door at the other end of the room.

To her relief, it opened into the entrance hall.

She felt wobbly and light-headed – especially when she remembered Ethan's sea-green eyes.

Must have really overdone it on the pirouettes, she thought.

CHAPTER TWELVE

Belle: Girls Just Wanna Have Fun

'It's not like Holly to miss dinner,' Belle mused as she and Cat left the dining room.

Cat sank into one of the big leather sofas in the entrance hall and propped her feet up on the table. 'Let's wait and see if she turns up. She probably just got carried away with her ballet!'

Belle could hear the stack of homework on her desk calling her name, but she was curious to know what Holly was up to – and she'd saved her a piece of pizza.

'OK, just for a moment then,' she agreed, perching on the sofa. After years of singing lessons and yoga, she'd got into the habit of sitting up straight. *Correct posture is essential for good singing technique,* her old singing teacher always said.

Suddenly Belle spotted Holly emerging from a door next to the dining room. She looked dazed and dishevelled, as if she'd been caught in a storm.

'Over here, Hols!' Cat yelled.

'What happened to you?' Belle asked.

'Oh, er, nothing . . . bit of a dizzy spell, that's all . . .' Holly murmured.

'Hmm,' said Cat suspiciously. 'So what were you doing in the kitchen storeroom, anyway?'

Holly flopped down in the middle of the sofa and put her trainer-clad feet up next to Cat's favourite zebra-print stilettos. 'Er . . . short cut!' she said.

There was definitely something odd about Holly this evening, Belle thought. She was usually so sensible and *grounded*. And what was that big splat of mud on her forehead?

'Are you feeling OK?' Belle asked, handing her the pizza she'd saved.

'Yeah, fine,' Holly replied absent-mindedly.

Belle noticed that she was already clutching a napkin-wrapped piece of pizza in her other hand. 'How did you get that?' she asked, but Holly wasn't listening.

'Feels like we've been here for ever, doesn't it?' she murmured dreamily. 'I can't believe it's only a week since we walked in through those doors – I thought the students sitting in here looked *so cool*. Now it's us!'

Cat laughed. 'Hey, *we're* cool!'

'Yeah, you bet!' Belle said. 'In fact, so cool, it's given me an idea . . .'

Belle's *awesome* idea had been burning a hole in her brain ever since the karaoke party. It had been so much fun, singing together with Cat and Holly. And judging by the cheers and calls for more, they had sounded pretty good too. So it was really an obvious move – *they should form a band*.

There was only one thing that had prevented Belle from sharing her idea with the other two before now: if she didn't score top marks in all her academic subjects, she would have to leave Superstar High!

Although Belle's father was a film director, he was dead set against her following him into showbiz. He said he'd *seen what the pressures of celebrity could do to people*, and he wanted Belle to train as a doctor or a lawyer. It had taken her months to persuade him to let her go to stage school rather than to a traditional boarding school. He had finally given in – on condition that Belle's grades at the end of the first term were all straight As.

Belle knew her friends thought she studied so hard because she was a natural-born egghead. They didn't know that her future at Superstar High depended on it. And that was why she couldn't afford to take time out to sing in a band.

But Belle had been *born to sing*! And they all wanted to be *performers*, didn't they? Surely they should get as much practice as possible. And Belle had always dreamed of forming her own girl group . . .

'Let's form a band!' she blurted out, unable to contain the thrill of the idea any longer. She would just have to set her alarm clock an hour earlier and *make* extra time.

'What? Us three?' Cat asked in amazement.

'Well, unless Victoria Beckham and Cheryl Cole just popped in . . .' Holly joked.

'Way-hay!' Cat shouted, stamping her feet up and down on the table.

Belle looked at her friends. They hadn't actually agreed. Perhaps they didn't want to be in a band. 'So, do you want to?' she asked nervously.

Cat and Holly exchanged looks. 'Of course we do!' Cat exclaimed. 'You didn't really think we'd say no, did you?'

Belle leaned back, suddenly feeling outrageously happy. She had two of the best friends in the world and they were all going to form a band!

Noticing that her gold Jimmy Choo sandals had somehow joined the other feet on the table, Belle started singing *Girls Just Wanna Have Fun*. Cat and Holly joined in, the three of them swaying from side to side in perfect time. As they finished the chorus, the girls clapped hands in a jubilant three-pronged high-five.

Belle was fizzing with joy. *We're really going to be a band!* she said to herself.

Then a fourth hand joined the high-five from behind the sofa.

A big, knuckly boy's hand.

Nick Taggart started trilling along in a high-pitched falsetto that even Belle had to admit was actually pretty impressive.

'So can I join the band?' he asked.

Belle looked at her friends for help. Surely they didn't want *boys* muscling their way into the band? Especially not Nick Taggart. He'd turn it into a comedy act!

Luckily Cat came to the rescue. 'It's – a – girl – band!' She spoke the words slowly, as if talking to a two-year-old.

'You know. For *girls*,' Holly added. 'The clue's in the name.'

'What do you mean, *girls*?' Nick pouted.

Cat giggled. 'Erm, d'you think there's maybe a

couple of things that your parents forgot to explain to you?'

Nick roared with laughter at that. Belle couldn't help joining in. Maybe he wasn't *quite* as annoying as she'd first thought. But she was still relieved he wasn't going to be joining the band!

She looked up and suddenly noticed that Bianca had come into the hall with Lettie and Mayu. They were leaning against the water-cooler, pretending to examine something fascinating on an iPod screen. It was obvious they were eavesdropping. Now Bianca looked up and grinned nastily.

'Ooh, look, Miss America is planning to start a band!' she taunted, fixing Belle with her laser-beam glare. 'It's the new Spice Girls – Spoiled Spice—'

'*Spoiled Spice?*' Bianca's words stabbed like a knife. Belle had almost got past worrying that everyone hated her because of her glamorous parents, but now the wound was re-opened. *Rise above it*, she told herself, but it wasn't working: *what if everyone really does think I'm spoiled?*

'Clumsy Spice,' Bianca went on, 'and Chubby Spice!'

Belle felt Cat flinch and momentarily forgot her own wounded feelings. Cat wasn't chubby! She just had a few more curves than most of the other girls. But that was a *good* thing – unless you wanted to be a high-fashion model! In fact, Belle knew from her mom that even super-models were getting fed up with the size-zero thing . . .

'Yeah,' smirked Mayu, pointing at Nick. 'And *Confused* Spice!'

'Young lady! How many times do I have to tell you?' The blood-curdling yell was accompanied by the unmistakable rattle of Mrs Butterworth, scooting across the hall in her swivel chair.

Belle, Cat and Holly guiltily snatched their feet off the coffee table. But, to their huge relief, neither they nor their feet were the target of Mrs B's wrath.

'Bianca Hayford! Yes, *you*, madam!'

Bianca's face switched from Snow-Queen white to glowing red.

'Park your backside on a chair if it needs a rest,' Mrs Butterworth scolded, skidding to a halt next to Nick Taggart. 'You'll break that water-cooler if you keep leaning on it like that!'

Bianca turned on her heel and flounced off.

'Ah, Miss Madison!' Mrs Butterworth exclaimed as she caught sight of Belle. 'I've just taken a phone message for you – from your father's personal assistant, dear. He'll be in London at the weekend. He'll meet you for tea at The Ritz on Sunday. How lovely!'

Cat and Holly were both smiling, looking slightly envious and very pleased for her, but all Belle felt was a wave of panic. There was only one reason she could think of why her dad would come to visit during term time. *He's changed his mind and decided to pull me out of Superstar High!* she panicked. Her dream of forming a band had been so close, she could almost touch it.

Now she was horribly afraid that it was over before it had even begun.

CHAPTER THIRTEEN

Cat: *Macbeth* and Original Material

Cat was in Mrs Salmon's Wednesday morning science class. Nathan – who'd appointed himself as her personal scientific adviser – had insisted they sit at the front. Belle was on her other side, frantically taking notes. The Fish (Holly's name for Mrs Salmon had stuck) was droning on: '. . . electric circuits, blah, homework must be in by tomorrow, resistors, volts, blah . . .'

Cat was busy arguing with herself about signing up for the *Macbeth* audition. She'd been thinking about it ever since they'd seen the poster in the Drama Department, and today was the deadline. *How can a newcomer like me hope to compete against all the older students?* she wondered. *But I so want to be part of it . . .*

At last the bell rang.

Right, Cat said to herself. *I've made up my mind*. She clapped shut her textbook and scraped back her chair.

'*One, two, three, eyes on me!*' Mrs Salmon slammed her

hands down on the desk. 'Did I *say* anyone could go yet?' The Fish's plump face had flushed from its usual shade of, well, *salmon-pink*, to a deep fuchsia.

One, two, three, eyes on me! Cat thought. *What was this, nursery school?*

'Catrin Wickham? Are you in a hurry to get somewhere more important?'

Cat decided that it was probably best not to answer that question truthfully. 'Er, no, miss. Sorry.'

Cat hurried to the Drama Department and found the *Macbeth* sign-up sheet. She imagined she was Keira Knightley signing autographs on the red carpet after another glittering premiere and began to sign with a flourish . . .

Kei— she wrote. Oops! She glanced over her shoulder to make sure no one had noticed, scribbled out ~~Kei~~ and wrote *Catrin Wickham*.

'Hello, Cat!'

Cat jumped as if she'd been caught with both hands in the biscuit jar. She whirled round to find herself nose to nose with Nathan. His hair was even more pudding-basin-like than usual today – like the detachable plastic hair of a PlayMobil figure. The way she described Nathan to herself, Cat thought, he sounded like a total geek-monster, but there was something oddly likeable about him.

'May I borrow your pen? I will sign up too.' Nathan had one of those soft voices you had to lean closer to hear, with just a trace of his native Spanish accent.

'Ah! Most commendable! Two exemplary students hitching their respective wagons to Mr Shakespeare's illustrious star,' Mr Grampian remarked, striding past with another huge tray of coffees.

Either he has a lot of friends or he has a serious caffeine habit, Cat thought. 'Don't ask me,' she laughed in reply to Nathan's blank look. 'I've no idea what he's on about either!'

Cat grabbed a cottage-cheese–and-celery sandwich from the dining room – since Bianca's Chubby Spice comment she'd switched from her usual cheese and salami – and joined Holly and Belle in one of the rehearsal studios in the new block, which they had booked for their first ever band practice.

Belle sat down at the piano in the corner and started to play the introduction to *Girls Just Wanna Have Fun.* The three of them improvised harmonies together while Cat picked at her sandwich (*Yuck! She hated cottage cheese and celery!*) and Holly figured out the controls on the state-of-the-art sound system.

Cat laughed. 'Whoa! You could fly a spaceship with all these flashing lights and buttons!' The world of technology was a total mystery to her, but luckily Holly seemed to know what she was doing and had soon hooked their MP3 players up to the speakers via the mixing desk.

'OK,' Belle said. 'Let's start by picking a variety of songs to sing along to – so we can get a feel for what works for us and what doesn't.'

Cat grinned at Holly, resisting the temptation to say *Aye-aye, Cap'n.* Belle could be a bit touchy on the whole bossiness issue – especially since Bianca's stupid Spoiled Spice comment. 'OK, as long as we start with *my* music collection!' she insisted. 'I've got some great stuff in here – Blondie, The Killers, the Foo Fighters . . .'

Holly pressed a button to start the first track and they began to sing.

Their voices sounded fantastic together, even though they were very different. Cat's voice wasn't perfect, she'd be the first to admit, and she couldn't always hit the high notes, but she captured the emotion in a song with a raw, bluesy sound. Holly had a sweet voice and a faultless sense of rhythm, which kept them in perfect time.

And Belle's voice? Well, Belle's voice was just un-be-liev-able! It was warm, powerful and subtle, with perfect pitch and the widest vocal range Cat had ever heard; it was hard not to be jealous!

After half an hour of rock, they moved on to Holly's selection of show tunes. 'Can we start with something from *Joseph*?' she pleaded. 'That was the first musical I ever saw. I was six!'

Cat smiled. 'Take it away, Hols!'

'How about *Any Dream Will Do*?' Belle suggested. 'I love that one!'

It wasn't the kind of music that Cat usually listened to, but she had to admit the songs were great fun to sing. And Belle gave her and Holly so many tips on how to get the most out of their voices that they were soon starting to sound really professional.

Cat laughed breathlessly. 'Wow! This is brilliant. We're going be the best band ever!'

'We *could* be a great band,' Belle said, her face suddenly clouding over, 'if we get the chance.'

'What do you mean?' Holly asked. 'This *is* our chance!'

'Oh, nothing,' Belle mumbled, sipping from her bottle of water.

Cat wasn't sure what she'd meant either, but Belle

wouldn't say any more. She was keen to keep practising, so Cat picked up Belle's iPod and started scrolling through the menu.

'Let's see what you've got on here,' she said. 'What shall we sing next?'

But before they could start, the bell rang for afternoon classes.

'Come on,' Holly urged. 'It's ballet. We don't want to be late for Miss Morgan – do we, Cat?'

Miss Morgan was waiting for them in the dance studio with the boys' ballet group in tow. But to Cat's delight, they weren't going to be doing ballet and Miss Morgan was only there to observe and to introduce a new, young and enthusiastic dance teacher. Sarah LeClair, she explained, had starred in several West End shows – until a badly broken ankle had ended her career as a professional dancer. *Hooray*, Cat thought. Not about the broken ankle, of course, but no ballet, no Miss Morgan and no butterfly-from-hell experience. Even better, they were working on jive – one of Cat's all-time favourite dances.

'OK, class!' Miss LeClair called. 'Finish your warm-ups and find a partner! Let's see how much jive you already know.'

Cat noticed Belle doing some very fancy footwork before the music even started – trying to position herself as far away from Nick Taggart as possible. Cat caught Holly's eye and grinned. They both thought Nick was hilarious, but Belle seemed to find his class-joker act confusing. She hadn't figured out yet that boys-doing-random-weird-stuff was just part of everyday school life – like lost property and detention.

Cat decided to help out: if Belle had to partner Nick on the dance floor as well as in the singing class, it could just drive her over the edge. 'Cat Wickham to the rescue!' she whispered to Holly as she charged across the room and grabbed Nick's arm.

As soon as *Rock Around the Clock* fired up, Cat realized that she and Nick were a great match – on the dance floor, that is! They jumped through catapults, yo-yos and pretzels with wild abandon.

Miss LeClair laughed. 'A little *too* wild perhaps!'

Zak and Holly were dancing up a storm. As usual, Zak looked as if he should have a surfboard in his arms, not a dance partner – but he was clearly one of the best male dancers in the year. Lettie and Bianca were jiving expertly with Frankie and Mason.

Meanwhile Belle was doing her best with Nathan,

who wore the petrified look of someone attempting to do a swing step with a man-eating tigress.

Nathan's a sweet guy, Cat thought, *but he isn't exactly Billy Elliot!* She couldn't imagine anyone she'd *less* want to rock around the clock with!

Cat was still humming *Rock Around the Clock* as she, Belle and Holly stopped at Mrs Butterworth's desk to return the rehearsal studio key.

'Been practising for the competition, have you, girls?' Mrs Butterworth asked, peering over her glasses.

'Sorry?' Cat asked. 'What competition?'

Mrs Butterworth scooted out from behind her desk and pointed to a new poster on the notice board.

TALENT COMPETITION

OCTOBER 20TH

WINNERS TO PERFORM AT THE

GARRICK SCHOOL, GALA CHARITY SHOWCASE

ORIGINAL MATERIAL ONLY

Cat laughed. 'We're not *that* crazy! That's only a few weeks away.'

'Indeed!' Mrs Butterworth smiled at her. 'It's really for the older students. They started practising before the summer holidays.' Then she executed a swift 180-degree spin in her chair and freewheeled back to her desk.

'Anyway,' added Holly, 'it says *original material*. We haven't got any of our own songs.'

'But why not?' Belle exclaimed suddenly. 'It's fun doing all the old songs, but is it really stretching us creatively?'

Cat exchanged a reality-check look with Holly. 'Er, Belle, we're in a band to *sing*,' she pointed out. 'If we wanted to stretch ourselves we'd have joined your yoga class!'

'Well, I think writing our own original material would be an awesome idea!' Belle's eyes had taken on a determined glint that Cat hadn't seen before. 'And the Gala Charity Showcase is a huge event. They have casting agents there and everything—'

'Exactly,' said Cat. 'This competition is a megamassive deal! It's not just some little school talent show with a couple of kids squeaking *Somewhere Over the Rainbow* and doing a few magic tricks.'

'But this could be our one big chance!' Belle sighed.

What's with the one-big-chance thing? Cat wondered. Was Belle planning to lose her voice at the end of term or elope with Nick Taggart?

'Well, I suppose there's no harm in *trying*,' Holly said diplomatically.

'*Thank* you, Holly,' Belle said. 'So, it's agreed? We'll each write a song and bring it to the next rehearsal.'

'Which is on . . . Saturday morning!' Holly gulped.

'Two days? To *write a song*?' Cat spluttered.

'How hard can it be?' Belle asked. '*If* you put your mind to it,' she added.

'Thinking about entering the talent competition, are we?' came Bianca's mocking voice from behind them.

Cat turned to see Bianca, Lettie and Mayu strutting past on their way to dinner.

'Looks like they're having *musical differences*,' Bianca went on, looking Cat, Belle and Holly up and down as if they were some form of insect-life.

'Sorry, I must have missed it, but did anyone actually *ask* for your input?' Cat snapped, feeling her temper spark. She knew she was meant to be *rising above it*, and saw the warning look in Holly's eye. But sometimes *rising above Bianca* was just too much of a challenge!

Bianca flicked her hair, but she was too taken aback by Cat's unexpected retaliation to come up with a response. Mayu wasn't, though. 'Ooh! Stress-yyyy!' she giggled in her little-girl voice. 'Come on, let's leave them to discuss their *artistic direction*!'

Mayu had cute little dimples in her cheeks and wore a pink mini-skirt with socks pulled up over her knees, but beneath the surface she was as sharp as a razor – *like a toxic Dolly Mixture*, Cat thought.

Bianca, Mayu and Lettie linked arms and continued to sashay towards the dining room.

'*Actually*,' Cat heard herself call after them, 'we've already got a brilliant song that'll blow the competition right out of the water!'

Holly and Belle opened their mouths, but both seemed to have lost the power of speech.

Bianca, Lettie and Mayu stopped and turned. Cat felt a delicious moment of satisfaction when she saw the astonished looks on their faces.

Then reality kicked in.

Oops! she thought. *I've really gone and done it now!*

CHAPTER FOURTEEN

Cat: Hot-water Bottles and Ninja Teachers

How hard can it be to write a song?

Well, think of the most impossible thing that you've ever done, Cat said to herself. *Or, more accurately,* not *done (because it's impossible, duh!). Then double it.*

It was Saturday morning, and Cat had been trying to get into the creative zone for two whole days. Belle had been spending hours working at the piano in the music room. Holly had been using some compose-o-rama computer program that she'd found when she was checking out the recording software for their harmony project. Cat was equally good at playing the piano and using computer programs – she couldn't do either.

To make things worse, she had planned to go home this weekend. She'd really been looking forward to it. Although she'd recovered from last Friday's attack of killer homesickness as soon as Belle and Holly had returned from the pool and cheered her up, she was still really missing her family. But she didn't want to let the band down, so she'd decided to stay at school and write her song.

She couldn't believe that she was the one who'd gone and told Bianca and her crew that they *already had a song*!

How smart was *that*!

Not for the first time, Cat wished she could learn to think things through before opening her mouth!

So here she was, sitting on a bench in the courtyard, looking for inspiration. She watched as Owen Mitchell and Tabitha Langley, two super-popular Year Eleven students, strolled past a bed of late roses, hand in hand, staring dreamily into each other's eyes. Yes, that was it: *a boy . . . a girl . . . flowers . . . young love* – what could be better? Cat was just beginning to feel musically inspired when Tabitha tripped and fell flat on her face.

Bianca and Mayu hurried past, both in heavy make-up and dress-to-impress outfits, talking loudly about a screen test for a TV advert they were attending. 'How's that amazing song of yours, then?' Bianca asked over her shoulder – narrowly avoiding stepping on Shreddie, who was right behind her as usual.

'*Peachy,*' Cat replied, flashing them a big cheesy smile. 'Just peachy, thanks . . . Give her up, Shreddie,' she whispered as the cat hopped up onto the bench next to her, staring longingly after Bianca. 'She's not worth it!'

OK, romance isn't working for me, Cat thought, turning back to her notebook. *What about a rebellious punk-style no-one-understands-me-because-I-am-young-and-tormented kind of song? I can really relate to that just now!* She scowled, thinking herself into the part of Angry Young Woman. She was Amy Winehouse with toothache. Fists clenched, brows furrowed . . . *I hate everybody in the world*, she scrawled, almost ripping the paper—

'Hi, Cat!' came a cheerful call.

Cat looked up, lips still curled in a ferocious snarl, to see Serena Quereshi and Gemma Dalrymple.

'We're going to Café Roma for lunch. Want to come with us?' Serena asked. Then she saw Cat's expression. 'Hey, are you OK?'

'Oh, erm, yeah, fine,' Cat mumbled, trying to arrange her face into a smile while holding onto her inner rage. 'Bit of stomach ache, that's all!'

'I've got this really great hot-water bottle you can borrow,' Gemma offered sympathetically. It was hard to imagine Gemma ever having aches or pains; she always looked as if she'd just stepped out of an advert for something ultra-healthy like pro-biotic yoghurt or muesli.

'Er, no thanks, it's probably just indigestion,' Cat replied. *Which probably isn't far from the truth*, she thought; all the celery she was eating these days was definitely not doing her stomach any favours.

'No worries!' Gemma smiled before heading off with Serena.

So much for anger, Cat mused. *It's hard to hate the world when the world comes up and offers you its favourite hot-water bottle!*

She suddenly noticed The Fish beetling across the courtyard in her white lab coat and her sensible shoes. *Oh, no!* Cat had been hoping to sneak last week's electric circuits homework into Mrs Salmon's pigeon-hole under a pile of papers so she'd find it on Monday morning and assume she'd overlooked it on Friday. What did teachers think they were *doing* coming into school at the weekend?

Mrs Salmon glanced down at her watch. Cat seized her chance. She leaped off the bench and bolted through a door at the back of the old school.

She found herself, heart pounding, in a small dark room that smelled of vegetables and old pasta. Ah-ha! This must be the short cut through the kitchen store-room that Holly had found. She just needed to find the door at the other end and she would come out next to the dining room. Cat took a step back, feeling her way along a rack of potatoes and . . .

Aaargh! Oomph!

. . . backed straight into a person.

Had The Fish somehow leaped, Ninja-like, into the storeroom ahead of her?

No, this was a tall, solid, man-shaped person.

A light flicked on.

The person was none other than James Fortune, retired heart-throb and principal of Superstar High.

'Oh, er, yes, h-hello!' he stammered, his hand on the light switch. 'Just checking the, er, *supplies*. You know . . .'

In the dark? Cat thought. She didn't say it though. He *was* the principal after all. He could lurk in a store cupboard whenever he liked.

Mr Fortune must have realized how feeble his excuse sounded, because he suddenly laughed. 'Actually, truth be told, I was avoiding someone,' he confessed.

'It wasn't Mrs Salmon by any chance, was it?' Cat asked.

'Er, yes, indeed it was.' Mr Fortune smiled wryly. 'She's been wanting me to look at a report recommending extra science tests every term, and I just haven't got round to it yet.'

'Snap!' admitted Cat. 'Science homework. *Tiny* bit late.'

Mr Fortune crinkled those famous blue eyes as he smiled at Cat across a shelf of cauliflowers. 'Ah, yes – Catrin, isn't it? Your mother's the Ewok? Well, coast should be clear now, I believe. After you!'

Cat stepped out of the cupboard, back into the courtyard, blinking in the sunlight, while Mr Fortune used the other door and disappeared into the entrance hall.

It was time for the band rehearsal and she was still no nearer to having written a song.

And she really was going to have to try and get her homework in on time in future!

CHAPTER FIFTEEN

Holly: *Twinkle, Twinkle, Little Star*

When Holly arrived at the rehearsal studio for band practice, Cat was already waiting. 'How did you get on with your song?' Holly asked.

'Rubbish!' Cat replied, holding up a dog-eared sheet of notepaper.

Holly laughed. 'Er, *I hate everybody*?'

Cat crumpled the page into a ball and drop-kicked it into the wastepaper bin.

'Me too,' Holly sighed, opening her laptop. 'I've got something, but I don't think it's going to be the next Number One!'

Holly pressed *play*. A few bars of synthetic-sounding piano and guitar tinkled out.

'Hmm, it reminds me of something . . .' Cat said, tilting her head thoughtfully to one side.

'*You're the One That I Want?*' Holly suggested hopefully. 'From *Grease*? That was the sound I was aiming for.'

'Erm, no. It's more . . . *Twinkle, Twinkle, Little Star,*' Cat replied.

Holly felt a twinge of disappointment. It had taken her ages to get to grips with the complicated song-composing program, and she hadn't thought her song was all *that* bad – although, listening to it now, actually it did sound a bit tinkly . . . Yes, Cat was absolutely right – *Up above the world so high* . . .

She burst out laughing. 'Yeah, but it *is* the disco re-mix!'

When Belle hurried into the room, Cat and Holly were singing a hip-hop version of '. . . *like a diamond in the sky,*' tears of laughter streaming down their faces.

'Sorry I'm late,' Belle puffed, pulling sheets of manuscript paper out of her leather portfolio. 'I was working on the harmony project with Nick. I know he's a total dingbat, but he's a genius with that recording software – and he's got much better vocal technique than I would have thought—'

'Woo-hoo! Sounds like you and Nick are really *harmonizing* these days!' Cat teased, still giggling.

'It's weird – he *does* have a really good voice when he stops goofing around long enough to use it,' Belle said vaguely.

Belle didn't even twig that Cat was teasing her,

Holly realized. In fact, Belle had seemed a little not-really-with-us for the last few days, and there was an anxious crease across her forehead. *She's working too hard*, Holly thought. *At least it's Sunday tomorrow. We'll have a nice lazy morning, and then she's seeing her dad at The Ritz for tea. That'll be a good break for her.*

Belle sat down at the piano, cleared her throat and began to play her song.

It started slowly. Then it suddenly went all jazzy, with lots of *doo-wah-diddly-bop-bops* up and down the scale. Then it turned into a ballad with a soaring gospel chorus and a disco beat . . .

The individual parts were cleverly written and beautifully sung. But, Holly thought, it was trying to be too many things at the same time. It was as if Belle had stuffed one of her beautiful Louis Vuitton suitcases so full of her designer clothes that she had to jump up and down on it to get it closed.

Belle ended on a glass-shatteringly high note.

There was a moment's silence.

'You didn't like it,' she sighed, her voice flat with disappointment.

'Er, you controlled that last note beautifully,' Holly said, trying to be tactful. 'Was it a high C?'

Belle looked expectantly at Cat.

Holly was trying to channel her thoughts into Cat's head. *Say something nice!*

Cat smiled. 'It was a bit over the top. In fact, that song was so far over the top that if it looked down with a telescope it wouldn't even be able to *see* the top!'

Oh, no! Holly thought. *Why does Cat have to be so honest all the time?*

Belle looked as if she was about to cry.

'What Cat meant—' Holly started, in an attempt to smooth things over.

'I *know* what Cat meant!' Belle said quietly. 'So let's hear Cat's song.'

'Er, I haven't written one,' Cat mumbled.

'Why not?' Belle asked.

'I got a bit distracted,' Cat replied. 'I had a secret liaison with Mr Fortune in a storeroom, for a start, and then—'

'You're just not taking this seriously,' Belle interrupted in a dangerously quiet voice.

'Just because I'm not tearing my hair out doesn't mean I'm not taking it seriously!' Cat spluttered.

Belle glared at her. 'You've *never* wanted us to do original material, have you? You didn't even *try* to write a song.'

'I *have* tried!' Cat shouted, looking as if she was

about to explode or burst into tears. 'I didn't even go home for the weekend because I was trying to write a *stupid* song for the *stupid* talent competition.'

Holly hated arguments. She had vivid memories of cowering in her bedroom while her mum and dad yelled at each other downstairs. That was years ago, and things were fine now that Dad had left and Mum had married Steve, but Holly still couldn't bear confrontations, especially between people she loved. She had to step in and stop it! She put her arm round Cat's shoulders and smiled at Belle. 'Hey, come on, you guys. Don't fight,' she said. 'Let's go and get some lunch.'

They marched in prickly silence to return the rehearsal room key to Mrs Butterworth.

Belle sighed pitifully as they passed the talent competition poster. '*Original material only*. I guess we won't be entering after all.'

'Bianca and her mates are going to just *love* this,' Cat groaned.

'You never know' – Holly smiled bravely – 'we *might* come up with something . . .'

'Don't hold your breath!' Cat muttered.

Belle turned on her heel and stalked off up the stairs.

'Oh, no!' Cat grimaced, clenching her fists to her

temples. 'I feel like a complete *maggot* now. I didn't mean to upset her. But that song *was* terrible.'

'I know,' Holly replied sadly. 'But there's something else bothering Belle at the moment. I just wish I knew what it was.'

CHAPTER SIXTEEN

Belle: Chocolate Macaroons and Lizard's Legs

Afternoon tea at The Ritz – Belle had been dreading it all week. She hadn't told Cat and Holly about her fear that she would be whisked away from Superstar High. Somehow she'd been fooling herself that if she avoided thinking or talking about it, the terrible threat might just go away. To leave the Garrick would be *unbearable*.

But as she stepped out through the front doors of the school, Belle felt as if a balloon was inflating in her chest, about to pop at any moment. She couldn't face it alone! She ran back upstairs and asked Holly and Cat to go to The Ritz with her. Cat was already on her way out and declined the invitation a little stiffly, but Holly jumped at the chance.

'Ooh, what shall I wear?' she cried. 'This is so-o-o exciting!'

'But you've lived your whole life in London,' Belle said in surprise. 'You must have been to The Ritz hundreds of times!'

Holly smiled. 'Walthamstow isn't really the bit of London that you see on the postcards. The nearest I've been to The Ritz is a packet of Ritz Crackers!'

As the taxi pulled away into Kingsgrove Square, Belle leaned back and closed her eyes. Her head was throbbing. On top of worrying about her dad, she was also feeling terrible about her argument with Cat yesterday. Would Cat ever forgive her for being so mean? 'I don't think Cat wants to be my friend any more,' she said softly to Holly.

'Of course she still wants to be your friend!' Holly exclaimed incredulously. 'It was just a silly disagreement. The only reason she's not coming with us is that she promised Nathan she'd practise for the *Macbeth* auditions with him.'

'But I said some really dumb stuff to her . . .' Belle went on.

'That's what friends are *for*,' Holly explained. 'They stick with you even when you do stupid stuff. *Especially* when you do stupid stuff, in fact!'

'Are you sure?' Belle asked doubtfully.

'I'm sure!' Holly said firmly, giving Belle's hand a quick squeeze. 'And you have to admit that none of us are exactly Andrew Lloyd Webber when it comes to songwriting.'

'I guess not' – Belle groaned – 'but I so wanted to enter that competition! It may just be my last chance—'

'What do you mean?' Holly asked.

Belle sighed and stared out of the rain-streaked window at the grey, crowded streets. She couldn't keep it bottled up any longer. 'I think my dad wants to take me out of the Garrick and send me to a "real school",' she said quickly, struggling to hold back her tears.

'What?' Holly gasped. 'But you only just got here!'

'I know, but he wants me to go to a proper school so I can be a brain surgeon or a nuclear physicist – anything as long as it's not a performer.'

'But why?' Holly asked.

'He's terrified I'll become some kind of drug-crazed, fame-hungry media-victim,' Belle explained.

'So we'll just have to convince your dad that the Garrick School is the Brainbox Academy for Studious Young Ladies.'

Belle smiled, but she wasn't at all sure her dad was going to be convinced by two members of the Garrick's newest girl band. *The band!* Belle made a mental note not to mention it.

When they arrived at The Ritz, Belle dragged her feet across the Palm Court restaurant in search of her dad's table as if she were on her way to the electric chair. She'd been here several times before, so she took little notice of the grand surroundings, but she couldn't help grinning when she turned to see Holly following in her slipstream, staring around at the domed glass ceiling, the gilded statues, the marble pillars . . .

'Oops, mind out!' Belle whispered, steering Holly away from a near-collision with a waiter carrying a tray of cakes.

Dad was sitting waiting. As always, his grey hair was immaculately groomed and he was wearing sunglasses and a beautifully cut grey wool Armani suit. He stood to greet Belle with a hug and a kiss.

'Dad, this is my friend, Holly Devenish,' Belle said.

'And what do you do, Holly?' he asked as they sat down.

'I'm a dancer,' Holly told him immediately.

Belle's heart sank as Dad made a 'Mmm' noise in his throat.

'But I'm also very interested in science and maths,' Holly piped up quickly. 'My mother's a teacher, so she really wanted me to get the best education possible.'

'But she's happy for you to go to a stage school?' Dad asked with a sceptical frown.

'Not just *any* stage school,' Holly reassured him. 'The Garrick has some of the best SATS results in the country – and it was rated Outstanding in its last inspection.'

Belle watched in awe as her father smiled and nodded and questioned Holly further. Now Holly was telling him about some 'Teacher of the Year' award that Dr Norris, their maths teacher, had recently won. This was going better than Belle could possibly have hoped! She'd had no idea that Holly would turn out to be her secret weapon in the campaign to prove that Superstar High was Brainiac Central.

'Well, you girls must be hungry,' her dad said eventually.

As Belle glanced down at the menu, she heard Holly gasp with delight. '*Chocolate* afternoon tea! That sounds like heaven on a plate!'

Dad signalled for a waiter and ordered chocolate afternoon teas all round.

As Belle kissed her father goodbye outside The Ritz, she was holding her breath. He'd still said nothing about wanting her to leave Superstar High; maybe she'd been worrying about nothing all along. But at the last second, as the taxi pulled up, Dad touched her arm and drew her to one side.

Belle swallowed nervously.

'Sounds like the Garrick's doing a fine job,' her father said, smiling. 'Work hard and have fun!'

Belle was so relieved she couldn't say anything, so she simply nodded instead.

Her father turned to Holly. 'Well, good to have met you,' he said warmly.

'Thank you for tea, Mr Madison,' Holly replied politely as she climbed into the taxi. 'And thanks for inviting me,' she added to Belle once they were both settled inside. 'I had the best time.'

'You earned it, Holly,' Belle told her with a grin. 'You *really* earned it!' She leaned across and gave Holly a Cat-style bear hug.

Holly laughed. 'You're welcome. I knew having a teacher for a mum would come in handy one day!'

Belle closed her eyes and leaned back against the leather seat. What a difference an hour could make! If she hadn't been held down by the seat belt, she felt as if she could float away on a cloud of happiness. The relief was almost overwhelming.

Her future at Superstar High was safe! At least for now.

'I'm not sure that last chocolate éclair was such a good idea!' Holly groaned, holding her stomach as they walked back to their rooms.

'Or maybe it was the five chocolate macaroons and the hot chocolate with chantilly cream and marsh-mallows that preceded it.' Belle stopped outside her room as she heard voices coming from the other side of the door:

'*Eye of newt and toe of frog, Wool of bat and tongue of dog . . .*'

Although Belle knew that the spooky voice belonged to Cat, it still sent an icy chill down her spine.

'*Macbeth*,' Holly told her. 'Second Witch.'

'*Lizard's head and owlet's wing—*'

'*Leg!*' said a boy's voice. 'It's lizard's *leg*, not lizard's head.'

'Grr! I'm *never* going to get this right!' Cat snapped.

'Don't worry, Cat. You will be the finest old hag in all the school.'

'Wow!' Holly whispered. 'I don't know who that is, but his voice sounds gorgeous.'

Belle knew exactly what Holly meant: the boy's voice was soft and earnest. Somehow he made being an old hag sound like a twenty-four-carat compliment.

'*By the pricking of my thumbs*' – Cat cackled – '*Something wicked this way comes. Open, locks, Whoever knocks!*'

'I think that's our cue,' Holly said, pushing open the door to see Cat standing in the middle of the room brandishing a celery stick.

Sitting opposite on a bean bag, holding a copy of *Macbeth*, was Nathan Almeida. He looked up at Holly and Belle and addressed them in the deep, stagy tones of an Elizabethan Scottish nobleman. '*How now, you secret, black, and midnight hags!*'

'Well, excuse *me*.' Holly put her hands on her hips, pretending to be mortally offended. 'And who exactly are you calling *hags*?'

Cat laughed. 'Don't blame Nate, blame William Shakespeare. It's the next line of the play.'

Belle smiled, but then she hesitated. She'd been so elated about her dad letting her stay at the Garrick that she'd forgotten about her disagreement with Cat. 'You're an awesome witch,' she said, hoping that Holly was right, and Cat really *was* still her friend.

'Thank you *very* much.' Cat said indignantly.

'Sorry, I meant that was awesome *acting*!' Belle explained.

'I know!' Cat grinned, jumping up and smothering Belle with one of her high-impact hugs. 'Look, I'm sorry about yesterday.'

'Me too.' Belle gulped. 'I had something on my mind – but, thanks to Holly, it's all OK now.'

'Have to go now! Things to do!' Nathan mumbled, suddenly bashful again, now that they had returned to twenty-first-century dramas. He hurriedly gathered his books together and slipped out.

As she closed the door behind him, Holly's foot brushed against something lying on the floor.

It was a large brown envelope bearing a printed label:

FOR BELLE, CAT AND HOLLY

CHAPTER SEVENTEEN

Cat: *Opposites Attract*

'Ooh, what's that envelope?' Cat croaked, her voice hoarse from cackling her Second Witch lines all afternoon. She was dying to hear all about The Ritz and what Holly had done to save the day, but that would keep for later. The envelope was too intriguing!

Holly passed it to Cat and collapsed onto the bean bag next to her. 'Can't . . . breathe . . .' she groaned. 'All internal organs replaced by chocolate!'

'Go on, Cat, open it,' Belle urged.

'Maybe it's a love letter!' Holly giggled. 'From a secret admirer—'

'Addressed to all three of us?' Cat said as she tore open the envelope and tipped out the contents. 'A really *greedy* secret admirer?'

A CD and a single sheet of paper slid onto the coffee table.

Cat turned the CD over; it was unmarked. The page,

however, was printed with music. 'It looks like a . . . song!' she breathed.

'Who's it from?' Belle asked, kneeling down for a closer look.

Holly shook the envelope and peered inside. 'There's no note.'

'Look,' Belle said, pointing to the corner of the page. 'I thought those letters were part of the music at first, but they must be the composer's initials.'

Cat looked. Belle was right. Two letters were printed at the end of the song: N.A.

'Well, we know who that is, don't we?' said Holly.

'We do?' Cat asked.

'N.A. – Nathan Almeida. It's obvious that he really fancies you, Cat—'

'Yeah, right!' Cat scoffed. 'I doubt Nate's even noticed we've *got* a band!'

'Well, let's see what the song's like,' Belle said, picking up the music and sliding the CD into her laptop. It was a backing track – a simple guitar arrangement with a drum beat underneath. She studied the musical score and picked out the harmony parts on her electric keyboard. After the first few bars she started to sing the words of the chorus:

'If opposites attract,
Why aren't you here with me?
And it's breaking my heart
That we're still poles apart.'

As Belle finished singing, Holly and Cat both burst into loud applause.

'That's an amazing song!' Cat said, looking really impressed.

'It's so romantic,' Holly agreed. 'And it shows your voice off perfectly, Belle . . .'

'. . . without going over the top,' Cat added.

'And the lyrics are great,' Belle commented. 'They sound as if they come straight from the heart . . .'

'. . . without being pass-the-barf-bag soppy!' finished Holly.

Cat played the CD again.

'Look – there's a high section here that suits Holly's voice,' Belle pointed out. 'And this part would be great for you, Cat . . .'

Bubbling over with excitement, they played the CD again and again, taking turns to work on their different parts.

'We are chalk and cheese,

The skies and the seas
Like bitter and sweet,
A trick or a treat . . .'

Cat looked at Belle and Holly. Their eyes were shining. They were back on track, the way they'd been before she'd had that stupid quarrel with Belle. It felt great! 'So I don't suppose anyone still feels like entering that talent competition?' she asked, putting on her doomiest, gloomiest voice.

Belle let out a delighted shriek and snatched up the music score in both hands. 'Thank you, N.A! Whoever you are!' she cried, planting a huge kiss in the middle of the page.

'Auspicious!' they all shouted in unison.

Just then, the door banged and Bianca stormed into the room. Lettie and Mayu were not far behind – not to mention Shreddie.

Now, what was it that Macbeth called the three witches? Cat asked herself. *Oh, yes, 'the black, and midnight hags'.*

'If you don't stop playing at pop stars in here,' Bianca spat, 'we'll report you to Miss Candlemas!'

'Yeah!' added Lettie lamely. 'We'll report you!'

Cat laughed. 'Ooh, I'm so-o-o scared!' Their housemistress was strict about some things – like boys having to be out of the girls' accommodation by nine p.m. and not letting the bath overflow – but she never stopped them having fun. In fact, she often joined in with any 'high jinks', as she called them.

Cat looked at Belle and Holly, who were both smiling and mouthing the words, *R-i-i-i-se above!*

'Well, some of us have been *trying* to revise for a maths test,' Mayu simpered.

And that, thought Cat as she climbed onto her bed and did her special *rise-above-it* soaring-eagle impression, *was highly unlikely*. The maths test tomorrow was on something even *she* found easy. And they'd obviously just been having an extreme makeover session next door: they were each wearing an entire Boots-counter worth of make-up and their hair was crimped to a crisp.

'Well, it's giving me a migraine,' Bianca complained, rubbing her temples and looking at Cat suspiciously. 'What *is* that music you keep playing anyway?'

'Oh, nothing you'd know,' Belle muttered, slipping the song-sheet under a book.

'Just some old, er, Ukrainian folk song,' Cat added quickly.

'Old Ukrainian folk song!' Lettie snorted with a disbelieving look.

'*Old Ukrainian folk song?*' Holly echoed after the Midnight Hags had set off down the corridor.

Cat giggled. 'I know, I know! It was the first thing that came into my head.'

'That's worrying,' Holly told her. 'Very worrying!'

'Come on, let's go to dinner,' Cat said. 'I'm starving. *Some* of us haven't been stuffing ourselves with cakes all afternoon!'

'And you never know,' Belle added. 'We might discover the identity of the mysterious N.A. while we're there!'

CHAPTER EIGHTEEN

Holly: Wild Flowers and Gangsta Rap

The mysterious N.A.?

About as mysterious as this tube of toothpaste! Holly thought as she got ready for bed later that evening – having hastily cleared up the mess that Bianca and her friends had left all over the floor after their makeover session, including several items of her own make-up that they'd pillaged from her drawer. Bianca's imaginary line down the middle of their room obviously didn't apply to Bianca herself!

Holly was convinced that the songwriter was Nathan Almeida!

One, Nathan's initials were N.A.; two, he adored Cat; and three, he was in the room just before the envelope appeared. The only mystery was why he hadn't just signed his full name in the first place.

Lucky Cat – she had a secret admirer. Even better, she had a secret admirer with a secret identity.

Nathan's just like Spider-Man, Holly reflected as she

climbed into bed. Not the running-up-tall-buildings-and-shooting-webs-out-of-his-wrists part, obviously. But, like Peter Parker, Nathan was the mild-mannered, geeky guy who transformed into a superhero. Nathan was Songwriter-Man!

Holly was strolling through a wildflower meadow. The setting sun was streaking the sky with peach and gold. The boy walking next to her slipped his hand into hers. It was Ethan Reed. 'Holly, I love your breathing!' he whispered.

She gazed into his limpid green eyes. 'Don't kiss me,' she murmured. 'I'm alive.'

A giant otter came scampering across the path. '*Eurgggh!*' it screamed. 'That is the grossest thing I have ever seen in my life!'

The otter sounded just like Furious Girl—

Holly sat bolt upright. She was in bed. It was Monday morning. It had only been a dream.

Only?

It was *only* the most embarrassing dream she'd ever had.

'Oh! My! God! It's revolting!' Now there was no mistaking Bianca's furious voice.

Holly opened her eyes, steeling herself for the worst.

A cockroach? A rat? Or had Shreddie mistaken Bianca's bed for his litter tray?

Bianca was standing in the middle of the room, clutching her industrial-sized make-up bag. Dangling from her fingers was a crumpled yellow napkin.

Not just *any* crumpled yellow napkin.

It was the crumpled yellow napkin from the pepperoni and anchovy pizza that Ethan Reed had given Holly after their collision.

Yes, she *had* kept it.

But, no, she *hadn't* kept it in Bianca's make-up bag.

She'd put the napkin in the bottom drawer of her bedside cabinet, along with her make-up and other odds and ends.

'Oh, er, yeah, that's mine,' Holly mumbled.

'So how did it get into *my* make-up bag? This is so-o-o not acceptable! There's gunk all over my Bobbi Brown shimmer blush! I do have allergies, you know!'

Allergies to paper napkins? Holly thought.

But she could guess how the napkin had found its way into Bianca's bag. Bianca and Lettie and Mayu had obviously thrown it aside when they were rooting through Holly's make-up yesterday afternoon. Holly must have scooped it up with Bianca's make-up when she was clearing up last night.

'Don't *ever* touch my stuff again!' Bianca bellowed. And before Holly could even begin to point out how hypocritical that was, she stomped off to the bathroom, slamming the door behind her.

Welcome to another fun-packed morning in room twenty-five, Holly sighed, flopping back down on her bed.

I think I'll go for another swim this morning, she thought. *And no, it's not just because Ethan is usually at the pool first thing! Everyone knows swimming is good for your core strength!*

In spite of her core strength, Holly's heart skipped a beat when she found that Ethan *was* at the pool, swimming backstroke lengths.

Holly couldn't help remembering her dream and blushing furiously when he came over to chat to her about tumble-turns and arm-extension. She nodded and shook her head, hardly uttering a word in case something ridiculous slipped out – *Don't kiss me, I'm alive*, for example . . .

Later, after a morning of geography and science, Holly grabbed a plate of pasta and pesto and sat down to lunch with Cat and Belle. Cat was checking her eyeliner using the back of a spoon as a mirror; Belle was studying her timetable. 'I'm going to book a rehearsal room this evening so we can work on the new song,' she said.

'Sorry,' Cat apologized. 'I'm going through Nathan's audition speech with him tonight. His Macduff still needs work.'

'What about we get together for half an hour and make a start?' Holly suggested quickly. Ever since the Great Original Material Dispute, she was getting good at picking up the trouble-ahead warning signs: a slight eyebrow-twitch from Belle; a defiant twinkle in Cat's eyes when Belle was planning her life for her. Time for Holly Devenish's International Peacekeeping Force to step in.

'Hey! Whassup, home-girls?' Nick Taggart shouted in an American street-gangsta voice, flipping a chair out from their table and draping himself over the back of it. 'MC Snoop Nicky Nick done wrote you ladies one buzzin' song!'

'*You* wrote us the song?' Cat gasped with a gob-smacked expression that Holly could read like a book; a book with very large print that opened with the sentence, *Could Nick 'Court Jester' Taggart be the secret song-writer who delivered* Opposites Attract *to our door last night?*

'So-o, how did you know that we needed a song?' Cat asked slowly.

'Belle told me,' Nick replied, forgetting for a moment that he was a hardcore gangsta from the mean streets of The Bronx, 'when we were working in the music library.'

Belle was very quiet.

Nick hollered across the dining room, 'Hey, my good bros, come help me out here!' Frankie, Zak and Mason swaggered over. 'We gonna lay down some sweet vibes for my ladies!' Nick told them once they'd finished exchanging convoluted handshakes.

'Wicked!' Mason whistled. Mason Lee, a tall Hong Kong Chinese boy with hair gelled into impressive porcupine spikes, was a talented percussionist. He picked up the rap beat with his palms on the back of a chair. Zak and Frankie joined in, screwing up their faces and making record-scratching sounds.

Nick pulled a piece of paper out his pocket with a flourish.

Cat grabbed it, and when she could stop giggling, started to chant the rap that Nick had written for her:

'They call me Cat 'cos I knows where it's at,
Non-stop, round-the clock, don't mock this rock chick
'Cos she's ready to paaaar-tay . . .'

Cat finished her verse and handed the paper to Holly.

Holly glanced at the words. It certainly wasn't *Opposites Attract!* Feeling a little self-conscious at first, she started the rap. After a few lines she was having so much fun she started throwing in some hip-hop dance moves. Zak joined her with a spectacular break-dance routine.

> *'Holly's the name, but I ain't so prickly,*
> *You want my love, better get here quickly.*
> *Check my smooooooth moves, in the groove, I ain't*
>   *sickly . . .'*

As her verse ended, Holly suddenly became aware that all the other students in the dining room had gathered round to see what the commotion was about. She sat down quickly and handed the paper to Belle. Belle started to back away with an expression almost identical to Bianca's greasy-paper-napkin-in-the-make-up-bag face, but everyone was now clapping along in time with MC Nick and the Crew – so, reluctantly, Belle took the paper and began to chant:

'*Belle of the ball, fairest of all, she so tall,*
Ding, baby, ding, you got that ring-a-ding thing,
Gotta believe her, she my diva, this girl can sing . . .'

As Belle finished, the three friends fell about laughing at themselves while the boys high-fived and the spectators gradually drifted back to their food.

That was fun, Holly thought as they filtered out of the dining room. Not exactly a masterpiece of song-writing, though. In fact, it had to rate as ten-year-old Gorgonzola on the Cheese-O-Meter. Surely a boy who rhymed *I ain't sickly* with *Ain't so prickly* couldn't have written *Opposites Attract*.

And anyway, Nick's surname was Taggart. His initials were N.T., not N.A.

Unless the A stood for—

'Hey, Nick,' Cat yelled back across the room to where he was now entertaining his 'fans' with Ali G impressions. 'What's your middle name?'

Cat's thought processes had obviously taken the same direction as Holly's.

Nick looked up and a deep blush flamed across his freckled face. 'What's it to you?' he shouted, gruffly pushing back his chair and heading for the door.

'Oo-ooh!' Cat grinned. 'I think we're on to something here!'

'No way.' Belle shook her head. 'No way is that buffoon our N.A.! *Ding, baby, ding? Ring-a-ding thing?* I rest my case!'

'Maybe that's what he *wants* us to think,' Cat suggested. 'That cheesy rap song could be a clever bluff. You know, to put us off the scent?'

'Baloney!' Belle retorted, coming to an abrupt stop in order to avoid bumping into Bianca, who had just come racing into the dining room. 'We're going to have to keep looking for our mystery songwriter,' she went on, stepping carefully round Bianca, who shot her an evil look. 'Whoever's secretly supplying us with songs, it isn't Nick. He's just not that smart!'

'Are you sure?' Holly asked. Then she noticed that Bianca was looking curiously at them, so she lowered her voice. 'After all, you did say he was a genius with the recording software . . .'

'Of course I'm sure,' Belle insisted, but a shadow of uncertainty passed across her face. 'Well, *pretty* sure,' she added.

Holly caught Cat's eye. Was it possible that Belle was starting to change her mind about Nick Taggart?

CHAPTER NINETEEN

Cat: *Twist and Shout*

Nick Taggart's a lot smarter than Belle gives him credit for, Cat thought as they left the dining room. And he was *way* more likely to be the Phantom Songwriter than Nathan was. Nathan didn't seem to like music, for a start. He'd even asked her to turn off The Killers when they were working on the electricity report! And he was really struggling with the harmony project—

Oh, no! The harmony project!

It was Monday! And Monday meant Mr Garcia's singing class. The singing class where they had to give in the CDs with the harmonies they'd recorded.

Cat and Holly had chosen their song. They'd learned how to record their voices onto the backing track. They'd worked out their harmonies.

There was just one minor problem – they hadn't actually *recorded* anything. That was supposed to have happened this lunch time. The one they'd just frittered away entertaining the entire school with an impromptu rap show.

Cat glanced at the clock in the entrance hall. They had ten minutes. If they ran straight to the recording suite and recorded both their voices simultaneously, they *might* just do it.

'Holly Devenish,' she said, 'I've got three words to say to you!'

Holly looked at her blankly. She'd clearly forgotten all about the assignment too.

'Twist! And! Shout!' Cat yelled.

'*Aarggghhhh!*' Holly screamed, clutching Cat's arm. Together they raced out of the hall, across the courtyard and into the recording suite – where Mayu was just closing her files on one of the computers, ready to head for the class.

'Mayu! Leave it switched on!' Holly panted. 'We'll lock up!'

'Oops! Sorry,' Mayu, said, curling her lip in a Cruella de Vil smile as she pressed the power button. 'Too late!'

'Grr!' Cat growled, stuffing their CD into the drive. Holly switched the computer back on, clicked frantically on the mouse and opened up their *Twist and Shout* audio file. Pulling on their headphones as the introduction started, they leaned into the microphone.

It was a Beatles concert and the fans were screaming . . . Cat pictured herself as John Lennon and Holly as Paul McCartney as they launched into the song . . .

'Sorry we're late,' Cat puffed as they barrelled into Mr Garcia's class at 1.35.

'Never mind, you're here now!' Mr Garcia rumbled. 'We're about to play the first CD. We're going to give each pair a mark out of ten for technical merit and originality. Let's get the ball rolling with . . . Bianca Hayford and Mayu Tanaka. Ah yes, *If I Were a Boy* by Beyoncé.

'I thought *you* were working with Bianca,' Cat whispered to Lettie.

'I was,' Lettie whispered back, 'but Bianca asked me to switch. Mayu's voice is much better than mine.' Her mouth drooped for a moment, but then she hurriedly added, 'But it's OK, I'm working with Mason Lee instead, and he's really musical.'

'Knickers, shush, will you?' Bianca hissed. 'I can't hear my song!'

'Please don't call me that,' Lettie whispered.

'OK, *Lettie*. Whatever,' Bianca replied hurriedly.

Over the next hour they listened to all the students' recordings. Frankie Pellegrini – who had an angelic singing voice, although he had the beat-up face of a junior boxing champion – had recorded a great version of a Westlife song with Zak Lomax, but Bianca and Mayu's *If I Were a Boy* was still easily the best. Mr Garcia picked up the last CD in the pile. 'Ah yes, Nick Taggart and Belle Madison – *Tragedy*, the old Bee Gees classic.'

Holly and Cat exchanged intrigued glances. Belle had kept this project Top Secret. But as soon as the song started, it was clear it was something very special. Nick sang the high parts in a perfect falsetto, blending skilfully with Belle's superb vocals in the lower range.

Mr Garcia led the class in a round of enthusiastic applause. Then he studied his clipboard. 'Hmm, there is one pair who have failed to submit anything: Holly Devenish and Catrin Wickham.'

Bianca turned and smirked triumphantly.

'Here it is, sir,' Cat said sweetly. 'We were just adding the finishing touches!'

Bianca's face fell.

Twist and Shout thundered out of the speakers. Cat looked across at Holly. Holly grinned back at her. It wasn't *quite* up to The Beatles standard, of course, but it really didn't sound bad at all. Although the tempo was a little too fast and there was an interesting *breathless* quality, it had drive and raw energy.

The class clapped and whooped as the track galloped to the finish.

'Mm! Nice *immediate* sound,' Mr Garcia murmured, 'and a great sense of *urgency*. Technically, though – let's just say the harmonies need some *refinement*!'

Mr Garcia examined his notes. 'It appears there's a tie for top score,' he said, 'between *If I Were a Boy* and *Tragedy*. I suggest we put it to a class vote.'

The result was overwhelming. Nick and Belle's *Tragedy* was the clear winner.

Nick threw his arms around Belle and planted a big sloppy kiss on her cheek. Cat waited for Belle to shove him away, but it seemed that in all the excitement she had forgotten that this was *Nick Taggart* kissing her! Only for a moment though. Soon she grimaced and rubbed her cheek. Cat caught Holly's eye and grinned.

'Hmmph! If I hadn't had that throat infection,' Bianca fumed, 'and all that trouble having to re-work the arrangement when Lettie let me down . . .'

'So-o-o-o,' Nick pleaded, turning to Cat and Holly, 'can I join your band now?'

'No way!' Cat laughed. 'Singing in a high-pitched voice still doesn't make you a girl!'

CHAPTER TWENTY

Belle: *Done Looking!*

Belle was still buzzing from the success of *Tragedy* almost a week later. What's more, band rehearsals were going fabulously and they now had a stellar song to perform for the talent competition.

She was still having to get up early every morning to fit in extra study time to make sure she got the A grades her dad expected, but she could live with that.

It doesn't get any better than this! Belle thought as she rolled up her yoga mat on Sunday afternoon, sipped her herbal tea with heather honey to protect her throat, and pulled on her favourite Manolo Blahnik boots before skipping off to a special invitation-only singing workshop with Larry Shapiro.

Yes, *the* Larry Shapiro! The world-famous vocal coach was running a series of workshops with a hand-picked group of Garrick students while he was in London working on a new musical. Larry Shapiro was only one of Belle's greatest heroes! He'd worked with everyone from Mariah Carey to Plácido Domingo!

Belle entered the studio and took a seat next to Frankie Pellegrini. Even Bianca's psycho death-stare couldn't spoil her mood today. *Although if looks could kill,* Belle thought, *I'd be a chalk outline by now and Bianca would be up for first-degree murder.*

When Larry Shapiro, tall and slightly stooping in a light blue suit, and wearing his trademark badly-fitting hairpiece, called for the first volunteer to demonstrate vocal control techniques, Belle's hand shot up. She was ready to sing her heart out!

Belle danced back up the grand staircase towards her room. She couldn't wait to tell Cat and Holly all about the workshop. Larry Shapiro said she had the makings of a world-class voice! There was Cat now, on her way across the entrance hall. 'Hey, Cat!' Belle called over the banister. 'Up here!'

Belle was still regaling Cat with her Larry Shapiro experience as they pushed open the door of their room. 'Wow!' Cat said, giving Belle a hug. 'That's brilliant— Ooh, what's this?'

A brown envelope lay on the carpet.

Cat picked it up, tore it open and pulled out a sheet of paper and a CD. 'Another song!'

The waft of chlorine that was becoming Holly's signature fragrance preceded her into the room. *She's been going swimming an awful lot lately*, Belle thought as she quickly moved the irises off the coffee table before they could be knocked flying by Holly's kit bag.

'Look, the Song Fairy's been again, Hols!' Cat laughed, waving the CD in the air.

'And it's signed N.A. again!' Belle added.

'*Auspicious!*' Holly and Cat chorused.

Belle studied the song carefully and played the CD track on her laptop. It was completely different to the last one. While *Opposites Attract* was a romantic ballad, *Done Looking!* was a lively song with a Latin American mambo sound:

> '*We're done looking! Now we're leaping!*
> *We won't stay in the shallows,*
> *Won't hide in the shadows,*
> *We'll take our friends by the hands,*
> *Take a chance, catch the wave, live our dream . . .*'

'Awesome!' Belle gasped when the three of them had sung the song – while dancing around the room to the infectious beat – for the fifth time.

'Having a little bop in here, are we, gals?' chuckled

Miss Candlemas as she called in to hand over a pile of clean sheets. All the girls had to strip their beds on Sunday mornings and make them up with clean bed-linen in the evening. Belle had never had to make her bed before coming to the Garrick, but she really enjoyed the novelty of doing all her own chores. Unlike Cat – whose side of the room always looked like a war zone!

'Just doing our Sunday laundry dance!' Cat grabbed a pillowcase and started improvising a little routine. Holly and Belle joined in.

'Wish I could stop and boogie with you myself – but, no rest for the wicked, eh?' Miss Candlemas laughed, shaking her head as she bustled off.

'So, now our mystery songwriter has struck twice and we still don't know who it is!' Holly said, dropping her pillowcase and frowning over the musical score.

'You know, this song describes exactly how we feel about this competition!' Cat said, flopping down on the pile of clean sheets. '*Take our chance! Live our dream!* Which means this N.A. guy must be someone who knows us really well! Like Nick Taggart!'

'No way!' Belle almost choked on her mineral water. 'It's definitely Nathan Almeida! Hel-*lo!* Latin

American song – Latin American guy! Anyone see the connection?'

Cat laughed. 'This is *Nathan* we're talking about! He's not exactly Ricky Martin, is he?'

'True,' Belle admitted, trying to pull her sheets from underneath Cat. 'But *Opposites Attract*? That's obviously about you and Nathan – you're outgoing, he's shy—'

'Right back at you!' Cat argued. 'You're cool, Nick's a screwball. Or at least he *pretends* to be. You're chalk and cheese, just like the song says.'

No way! Belle thought. She couldn't deny that she and Nick were opposites. And she had definitely started to get on with him a lot better since the success of the harmony project. But as for being attracted? *Never going to happen!*

'What makes you so sure the writer is even a boy?' Holly said thoughtfully.

Belle stared at her. She'd never considered that N.A. could be a girl.

'Nah!' Cat said, after giving it a moment's thought. 'Why would a girl want to be anonymous? There'd be no reason to be embarrassed about it, like a boy would be . . .'

That was a good point, Belle thought. 'And I can't

think of any girls with the initials N.A., can you?' she added.

'No,' Holly admitted. 'Cat's probably right. But we need some hard evidence before jumping to conclusions that it's Nick – or Nathan . . .'

Holly is so sensible and fair-minded, Belle thought admiringly. *If she wasn't going to be a dancer, she'd make a great lawyer.*

'Yeah! Let's raid their rooms and look for clues,' Cat suggested excitedly. 'Like *The Famous Five*.'

'Or maybe not,' Holly said. 'What about trying to find out what Nick's middle name is first!'

Cat grinned. 'Remember how embarrassed he looked when I asked him? I bet it's because it begins with A and he doesn't want us to work out that *he's* N.A.!'

'N.A. is so *not* Nick Taggart, but just to be sure, I'll find out what his middle name is,' Belle offered. *It'll be easy enough*, she thought. *All I have to do is sneak a peek at the mail in his pigeonhole. One of the envelopes is bound to have Nick's middle name on it – or at least his initial.* She was quite sure it would start with something other than A.

'And *you* could work on Nathan, Cat,' Holly suggested.

'How? I can't just beat a confession out of him,' Cat protested.

'No beating required. Just use your feminine charms!' Belle told her. 'It's pretty obvious he fancies you.'

'Hmm. I'm not so sure, but I suppose I could try and, you know, flirt with him a bit or something,' Cat said thoughtfully.

'Awesome idea! You work it, girl!' said Belle.

'So, Belle, are you going flirt with Nick to find out his middle name then?' Cat asked, with a mischievous look.

Belle laughed. 'Wait and see. I have my ways!'

'OK, it's a plan!' Holly clapped her hands. 'Cat's on Advanced Flirting Duty with Nathan. Belle's on Undercover Reconnaissance with Nick – and I've got a funny feeling I've seen the initials N.A. somewhere else as well, so I'm going to try and track down where.'

'We'll have the Mystery of the Secret Songwriter wrapped up in no time!' Belle predicted.

'But let's go down to dinner first,' Cat suggested. 'It's dangerous to flirt on an empty stomach, you know!'

CHAPTER TWENTY-ONE

Cat: Magnetism and Mambo

After dinner Cat hurried back to her room to change into her best flirting outfit. She pulled off the baggy jumper she'd taken to wearing a lot since Bianca's Chubby Spice comment. *The one advantage to all this dancing and celery*, she thought, looking at herself critically in the mirror, *is that I'm definitely losing weight.*

Feeling buoyed by this, she rummaged through her wardrobe and selected a slinky black mini-dress, black tights and her favourite zebra-print high heels. Then she applied extra eyeliner, pinned her hair into a romantic tangle with a few artistically arranged trailing curls, and set off for Nathan's room in a cloud of Obsession.

She reached the end of the corridor, then ran back, grabbed a couple of random science books from her desk, and set off again.

The boys' rooms were in the new block next to the pool and the sports centre. Cat had ventured along these corridors only once or twice before. She wrinkled her nose at the odour of slightly stale boy. The girls' corridors didn't exactly smell of sugar and spice and all things nice – more a mixture of shampoo, talcum powder and chocolate – but at least it wasn't crisps (assorted flavours), old sweat and weapons-grade deodorant. She passed the room that Nick Taggart shared with Zak Lomax. Rock music thudded out from behind the closed door.

Cat knocked at Nathan's door just as his roommate, Frankie Pellegrini, was heading out for the gym. Frankie whistled softly as his eyes drifted across her low-cut dress. Nathan looked up from the laptop screen on his desk. 'I've found some excellent websites on the fundamental principles of magnetism,' he said, seemingly oblivious to Cat's *femme fatale* look. 'It *was* magnetic fields you wanted to revise, wasn't it?'

'Oh yes,' Cat purred. 'You know, magnetic attraction . . .'

She was a glamorous Russian secret agent seducing James Bond into revealing the location of the nuclear missile . . . She sat down on the edge of Nathan's chair, wriggled a little closer and—

'Here, I'll get Frankie's chair for you,' Nathan offered, jumping up and almost knocking Cat off her perch. Once he'd installed her next to him on another chair, he settled down in front of the computer again.

Cat leaned across and placed her hand over Nathan's on the mouse. 'So,' she said, 'the thing about magnets is that *opposites attract* . . .?'

'That's correct,' Nathan agreed, nudging Cat's hand gently aside and clicking with the mouse. 'If you study this diagram here, you'll see that there are two poles—'

'We're a bit like that, aren't we, Nate?' Cat said, smiling coyly. '*You and I* . . .'

'Like what?'

'Opposites! You're all *shy* and *thoughtful* and *deep*, and I'm . . . not . . .'

Nathan nodded. 'Well, yes, that's probably why we're such good friends.'

'*Very* good friends!' Cat simpered. 'The kind of friends who might want to help each other, you know . . . secretly?'

'No, it's OK,' Nathan replied, looking slightly puzzled. 'I'm happy to help you with homework any time, and I don't mind *who* knows about it.'

This is Mission Impossible, Cat thought. *He hasn't got a clue what I'm talking about.* In a last-ditch attempt, she changed tack. '*Done looking, now we're leaping!*' she announced. She gazed into his eyes for a spark of recognition – eyes which, she noticed for the first time, were dark brown with gold flecks . . .

Nathan frowned and pulled off his glasses. 'Have I got something stuck on the lens?' he asked, squinting at them.

Phew, that's a relief! Cat thought. *I thought he was going to kiss me for a moment.* Not that there was anything *wrong* with Nathan, of course. He was a great mate. Just not boyfriend material!

'So, Nate, do the letters N.A. mean anything to you?' she asked, giving up on the flirting and going for the direct approach.

Nathan frowned as he replaced his glasses. 'Well, they're my initials, but—'

'What about anything else or any*one* else?' Cat demanded.

Nathan scrunched his brows up in thought. 'Let's see, N.A. . . . Oh, yes!'

'What?' Cat asked excitedly. Maybe she was wrong. Perhaps he was about to crumble and confess to being the Phantom Songwriter . . .

'Na is the symbol for the chemical element sodium.'

My work here is done, Cat said to herself in her best Russian-agent accent.

Although it wasn't, because she really *did* need help with understanding those magnets. 'Sorry, can you just explain that thing about the poles again?' she asked.

'Of course,' Nathan said, smiling happily. 'It's quite simple really. If you look at this chart . . .'

The next band practice was on Tuesday evening. Holly had spent the last few days working out a mambo-style dance routine for *Done Looking!* Bands were only allowed to perform one song in the talent competition and, after some argument, Cat and Holly had persuaded Belle that they should choose the lively, energetic Latin American number rather than the slow, romantic *Opposites Attract.*

Holly started up the *Done Looking!* backing track on the sound system in the rehearsal room and walked her friends through the steps – which involved lots of hip-swinging and quick-stepping, with cute little jumps on the *Now we're leaping!* hook-line.

'Holly Devenish! You are brilliant!' Cat collapsed on the floor, panting with exhaustion after the third run-through. Singing while dancing such an energetic routine wasn't going to be easy, but Cat was sure that it would really wow the judges if they could pull it off.

Belle was a little hesitant at first. Cat could see that

the extravagant Latin American style wasn't her natural habitat. But Holly was a patient teacher, and she simplified some of Belle's moves. 'After all, Belle's singing the lead vocals,' she said tactfully, 'so it's not fair to expect her to do as much on the dance side!'

By the end of the rehearsal, Cat was leg-achingly exhausted. But it was a good feeling. Things were really starting to slot into place. And they were all beginning to feel the excitement.

The talent competition was only a few weeks away!

'So,' Belle said as they walked back across the courtyard after the rehearsal, 'we've got another big decision to make. We need a *name* for our band!'

'I've been thinking about that,' Cat said. 'What about something beginning with N.A. – you know, in honour of our secret songwriter?'

She waited for Belle to argue, but to her surprise, she agreed immediately. 'Hey, great idea!'

'Hmm. What about . . . er . . . Next Answer?' Holly suggested.

'Too boring!' Belle said. 'Naturally Auspicious?'

Cat laughed. 'Too long! How about . . . Nervous Attack?'

'Too scary!' said Belle.

'Nibbling Anteaters?' Holly ventured. 'Noisy Alligators?'

'Too weird!' Cat and Belle said together.

'*Aarggh!* We'll be stuck with the Chlorine Doreens if we don't think of something soon,' Holly groaned.

'Hey, girls, need some help?'

Cat turned to see Nick walking behind them, with Zak. 'We need a name for our band,' she said. 'And it's got to start with the initials N.A.'

'Er, why?' Nick asked.

'Because we say so,' Cat retorted with a grin. 'So no arguments!'

'Whoa! That's rad, man!' Zak exclaimed. 'No Argument!'

'Mm, not bad . . .' Holly said.

'I've got it!' Nick shouted, punching the air. 'Nick's Angels!'

'*Nick's Angels?*' Cat laughed as Belle emitted a very uncool, un-Belle-like snorting sound that was somewhere between horror and amusement.

'You know, like *Charlie's Angels*,' Nick explained. 'That was three gorgeous girls. Charlie was their boss. I could be, like, your *manager*.'

'Ha ha! Very funny!' Belle scoffed, not even remotely

close to amusement now. 'We don't need a manager. And we are certainly not *your* angels!'

'Yeah. We're *nobody's* angels, thank you very much!' Cat laughed, poking Nick in the ribs.

Then she suddenly stopped laughing, replaying what she had just said in her head.

She looked at Holly and Holly looked at Belle. There was a long freeze-frame pause and then . . .

'That's it!' Holly said.

'We're Nobody's Angels!' all three girls shouted in unison.

CHAPTER TWENTY-TWO

Holly: *Dirty Dancing* and Stormin' Norma

The following Sunday morning Holly was singing to herself and dancing a few steps as she crossed the entrance hall. She'd gone with Miss LeClair and a group of other students on a trip to see *Dirty Dancing* in the West End last night – and she couldn't get the music out of her head. *One day*, she daydreamed, *that will be me up there on stage, singing and dancing . . .*

She stepped out through the front doors and blinked in the bright sunlight. A group of boys in football strip were standing around at the bottom of the wide stone steps.

One of them was Ethan Reed.

Holly paused on the top step. She immediately forgot all about West End musicals. *This* was her big chance to prove to Ethan that she was not a total dimwit. She would walk down the stairs calmly and sanely; no head-butting or spouting gobbledygook this time. Luckily she was on her way out to meet Belle and

Cat at the Café Roma on the other side of Kingsgrove Square for brunch, so after her swim she'd changed into her favourite jeans and even slicked on some lip gloss.

Well, here goes. Step down, two, three . . .

Ethan looked up and flashed his high-voltage smile. 'Hi, Hol—' he began

'About flippin' time too, Baddeley!' yelled one of the boys. 'We'll be late for the match!'

Holly turned, just in time to see Felix Baddeley hurtling out of the door behind her . . .

. . . and tripping on his boot-lace. He teetered for a moment before tumbling in a tangle of limbs and shin pads . . .

. . . and crashing into Holly.

In that split second Holly realized that if she fell down all six steps, she would probably break her ankle at the very least. *You can't dance with a broken ankle. Just look at what happened to Miss LeClair!* There was only one option.

As her legs started to crumple, Holly bent her knees, pushed off and jumped, launching herself in a sideways dive.

This could go one of two ways, she thought as she watched the terracotta pots with their little star-shaped trees speed past. *Either Ethan will reach out and catch me . . .*

. . . or I'll crack my head open on the pavement.

At the top of her trajectory, Holly's brain cut out and her body switched to Dance–Mode Override. Her legs extended and her toes pointed. Her arms swept up elegantly into fifth position. Her face arranged itself into the big smile that dancers always wear to mask the pain.

And she landed in Ethan's arms.

Her momentum took him by surprise and he almost dropped her. But just as her braids brushed the ground, he summoned up his strength and swept her up again. Holly twisted round in his arms and sprang away with a half-turn to land perfectly at his side. She stretched out her arms like a gymnast dismounting from the beam.

Felix, who was now lying at her feet, winded but apparently uninjured, held his hand up for a knee-high high-five. 'Way cool!' he whistled. 'That was like *Swan Lake* meets *The Matrix*!'

Ethan was grinning at her. The rest of the footballers were staring, open-mouthed.

Holly felt as if she were back in one of her dreams. She had just jumped into Ethan's arms! She felt as if she were still soaring through the air.

'Sorry I'm late, Ethan,' Felix groaned. 'I got waylaid by Stormin' Norma about some stupid permission slip for the away match—'

'*Stormin' Norma?*' Holly couldn't help asking.

Ethan laughed. 'Mrs Butterworth. We've always called her that since we found out her name's Norma.'

'Yeah, either that or The Chairminator!' Felix added.

But Holly wasn't listening. She was picturing Mrs Butterworth sitting behind her desk on the first day of term with a name-badge stuck on the lapel of her bristly tartan jacket: MRS N. A. BUTTERWORTH, SCHOOL SECRETARY.

At last she remembered where she'd seen the initials N.A. before!

Holly ordered a large cappuccino and a chocolate brioche and took a seat next to Cat and Belle at the back of Café Roma. They were poring over an official-looking form.

'Looks boring!' Holly said, still smiling. She hadn't really come back down to earth yet, but decided she'd tell Cat and Belle about the Ethan stair-jump *later*; she wanted to keep it as her own treasured secret for just a little longer.

'Entry form for the talent competition. We've got to

hand it in to Mr Garcia tomorrow,' Belle explained. 'Along with a copy of the musical score for the backing band.'

Holly examined the form. Cat and Belle had filled out most of it already.

NAME OF BAND/GROUP/ PERFORMER:	*Nobody's Angels*
MEMBERS OF BAND/GROUP:	*Belle Madison,* *Cat Wickham,* *Holly Devenish*
NAME OF SONG:	*Done Looking!*
NAME OF SONGWRITER:	

'Name of songwriter?' Holly said. 'But we still don't know who N.A. is!'

'No,' said Cat, 'but it's not Nathan Almeida! I turned the Flirt-O-Matic up to Maximum, and all I got was the chemical symbol for sodium.'

'I haven't found out about Nick's middle name yet,' Belle sighed. 'I've asked his buddies and looked at his mail, but no luck.'

'At least we can rule out the N.A. I was trying to remember,' Holly said. 'Turns out it's Norma A. Butterworth!'

Cat howled with laughter. 'I can't see Mrs B as our secret songwriter! She'd have to get out of her chair to come up to our room for a start!'

Croissant crumbs scattered across the table. Holly was pleased to see that Cat seemed to have given up on the strict cottage-cheese-and-celery diet she'd been following since Bianca called her *chubby*.

'Well, we'll just have to leave the form blank for "songwriter" and hope the organizers accept it, I guess,' Belle said. 'Unless . . .' she added thoughtfully.

'Unless what?'

'I've had an idea.'

'Uh-oh!' Cat grinned and held her head in her hands. 'Not another of Belle Madison's Legendary Awesome Ideas. I seem to remember that it was one of your awesome ideas that got us into all this in the first place!'

'Well, the last two songs have been delivered under our door on Sunday evenings,' Belle continued, ignoring Cat's remark. 'Today's Sunday. We could hide in our room and—'

'Keep watch in case we get another visit,' Cat interrupted. 'Genius!'

'It's awesome!' Holly agreed, feeling a thrill of excitement. 'Operation Song-catcher is *go*!'

CHAPTER TWENTY-THREE

Holly: Operation Song-catcher

Operation Song-catcher commenced at seventeen hundred hours precisely; after Belle had checked they'd all made a 'bathroom visit'. There was no keyhole but the crack between the door and the frame was just wide enough to glimpse a narrow strip of anyone outside in the corridor.

They turned off the lights and got into position. Holly took first shift, kneeling with her eye pressed to the crack, while Cat lounged on a beanbag and Belle did yoga exercises to pass the time.

Now all they had to do was wait . . .

. . . and wait

. . . and w a i t . . .

Holly checked her watch. It had only been ten minutes!

'What if they're wearing a disguise?' Belle whispered from her lizard pose.

'Ooh yeah! Like Zorro,' Cat said, 'or Batman—'

'Sshh!' Holly hissed. 'I can hear something!'

She held her breath. Footsteps were coming along the corridor. The light coming through the crack was blocked by a leg. Holly could hear scary-shark *Jaws* music in her head.

There was a knock at the door.

Checking there's no one here! Holly thought.

Then an envelope appeared under the door. Holly felt her heart thump against her ribcage. The envelope-slider stepped back and she caught a glimpse of black jeans and trainers. *It was Nathan Almeida!*

Holly turned slowly, her eyes wide with amazement. 'I saw him!' she squeaked. 'It's—'

'Nathan. I know.' Cat grinned, holding up the sheet of paper she'd already ripped out of the envelope. '*Dear Cat,*' she read aloud. '*Here's a list of some magnetism websites you might find useful—*'

'Sshh!' Belle whispered, taking up position for the next shift at the door. 'The real songwriter could come along at any minute—'

Suddenly Holly jumped. What was that scratching noise at the door?

'Cat!' Belle whispered, her eye still glued to the door.

'What?' Cat whispered back.

'No, it's *the cat,*' Belle breathed, quickly opening the

door and scooping Shreddie inside. He glared at them all disapprovingly before curling up on Cat's bed to wash his paws.

Cat took her turn, then Holly again. She was starting to think the Phantom Songwriter was never going to turn up when she heard footsteps approaching. Could this be it?

'False alarm!' Holly sighed a moment later. 'It's only Bianca with Mayu and Lettie. They've just gone into our room.'

Shreddie must have heard Bianca's voice too. He jumped down from the bed and started miaowing at the door, desperate to see his True Love.

Cat picked him up and cuddled him. 'Shreddie, you are one mad cat,' she whispered into his fur.

Holly stood up and stretched her legs. 'Your turn, Belle,' she said.

But Belle — now in downward-facing dog pose, with her eyes only centimetres from the carpet — was staring, transfixed, at the gap under the door. Holly followed her gaze. The corner of a brown envelope was sliding slowly towards them. As quickly as she could, Holly crouched down again in lookout position—

But at that moment Shreddie scrabbled frantically out of Cat's arms.

Cat screamed. Holly jumped and banged her head on the doorknob. Shreddie leaped onto the coffee table, knocked over the irises and pounced on the envelope.

But it had already been snatched back from the other side of the door.

Feeling slightly dizzy, Holly opened the door. The corridor was empty. And silent.

'Oh, no! We've scared them away!' she groaned.

'So we still don't know who it is – and even worse, they'll probably never write us another song after this!' Cat grumbled, kicking a bean bag. 'Whose brilliant – or should I say *awesome* – idea was this?'

'I'm really sorry,' Belle said sadly. 'I thought it would work.'

'It's not *your* fault!' Holly sighed, disappointment descending on her like a cold wet blanket. 'We *all* thought it would work.'

'Yeah, Holly's right. I'm sorry,' Cat said. 'It *did* seem like a good idea at the time!' Then she broke into a smile. 'What are you like, Hols, hitting your head on the doorknob? Are you OK?'

Holly laughed, rubbing the bruise. 'Yeah . . . It *was* pretty funny when Shreddie knocked over the vase of flowers. He's even clumsier than I am!'

'Maybe he's secretly in league with Bianca,' Belle said as she started mopping water from the table, 'and he did it deliberately to mess up our plan!'

Holly made a heroic attempt to look on the bright side. 'Well, no good crying over spilled water! At least we tried. We'll just have to put the initials N.A. on our form and hope that it's enough.'

As Belle was carefully putting the entry form for Nobody's Angels into Mr Garcia's pigeonhole, Holly had an idea. She took a pen and notebook from her bag and wrote a message:

Dear N.A., We are very sorry for trying to catch you out earlier. We won't do it again. Thank you for everything.
Love from Holly, Cat and Belle

She folded the note over, wrote *N.A.* on the front and placed it in the pigeonhole for students with surnames beginning with A.

Maybe, just *maybe*, the songwriter would find it, forgive them and come back again.

CHAPTER TWENTY-FOUR

Belle: Laundry Lists and Middle Names

Belle was worried.

It was a blustery Thursday morning and she was finishing her early morning run around the school grounds. She had an English essay on her desk waiting to be finished, but that wasn't the problem. She checked the integrated stop-watch-and-heart-monitor gadget on her wrist; she'd been a little slow, but *that* wasn't the problem either.

Belle was worried about the talent competition. Would Mr Garcia accept their entry, even though they'd not filled in the full name of the songwriter on the form? Or would Nobody's Angels be disqualified before they'd even started?

Belle slowed as she passed the back of the sports centre. Miss Candlemas was taking delivery of clean sheets and tablecloths from a laundry van. 'Ooh, Belle!' she called. 'Be a love, and' – Belle removed the earpiece of her iPod and strained to hear over the squally breeze

– 'pop along to Mrs B's office and bring me the laundry list off her desk. She's late this morning – here's the master key.'

Belle caught the key and jogged around the new buildings, across the courtyard and into the entrance hall. Mrs Butterworth's office or 'inner sanctum', as she called it, was behind the big desk in the reception area, next to the pigeonholes – so she could easily scoot between the two. But now the black leather swivel chair sat empty behind the reception desk.

Belle knocked and then turned the key in the lock. She soon spied the laundry list on the desk in a tray marked OUT. She picked it up, but as she was turning to leave, she glimpsed something out of the corner of her eye. Between the out-tray and a spider plant was a pile of papers.

The top page was headed, *Almeida: Nathan Alejandro*. Below the name were typed the words: *Science Test*.

Ooh, Belle sighed, *what I wouldn't give to see* my *test result. Maybe just one little peek*, she thought, inching towards the papers, but then she paused. Mrs Butterworth could turn up at any moment and if she was caught snooping, she was pretty sure it would be game over for her at the Garrick.

She forced herself to leave the test papers

untouched, but just as she was about to go, she realized something that set her pulse racing so fast she thought her heartbeat monitor might explode: Nathan's middle name was Alejandro! And if *Nathan's* middle name was on his test . . .

Swiftly Belle lifted the stack of papers about where she thought the Ts should be.

And that's when she heard the unmistakable sound of Mrs Butterworth's chair rattling towards her office.

She was going to be caught red-handed!

'Belle!' cried Mrs Butterworth. 'Whatever are you doing in my office?'

Belle didn't have time for finesse. With a swipe of the arm she knocked the spider plant and the stack of test papers cascading to the floor. 'Oh, no, I'm sorry!' she gasped. 'Miss Candlemas sent me to get the laundry list. You made me jump and—'

'Hm!' Mrs Butterworth frowned and peered at Belle over her glasses. 'This is really *not good enough . . .*'

'I'm so sorry. I'll pick everything up,' Belle said, throwing herself to the floor and beginning to scoop up the papers, all the while frantically trying to spot Nick's test and read his middle name without the school secretary noticing.

'No, leave them, dear,' said Mrs B, wheeling her

chair towards the desk. 'I'll be having *words* with Miss Candlemas. Giving my office key to a student when there could be all kinds of confidential documents in here . . .'

Belle backed out of the office, leaving Mrs Butterworth to tidy up. Once safely in the hall, she sank down onto the bottom stair to catch her breath and smiled for the first time since the dramatic failure of Operation Song-catcher last night. Because she'd caught sight of the name she was looking for: *Taggart: Nicholas Umberto.*

No wonder he'd been embarrassed about his middle name. And she'd been right all along. Nick Taggart was *not* the Song Fairy!

Belle skipped lunch to finish her English essay. Then she ran to Mrs Butterworth's desk to pick up the key for the rehearsal room she'd booked for a band practice. Belle expected the school secretary to scold her after this morning's Office Break-in Fiasco. But Mrs B only seemed concerned about her health. 'How are you feeling now, dear?' she asked.

'Er, fine, thanks,' Belle stammered, wondering if she looked pale.

Mrs B smiled. 'Oh, good. Well, one of the other girls

has taken the key.'

Holly or Cat must have picked it up already, Belle thought, racing over to the rehearsal rooms.

But when she opened the heavy sound-proofed door of the studio, it wasn't Holly and Cat adjusting the sound system and plugging in the microphones; it was Bianca Hayford and Mayu Tanaka.

CHAPTER TWENTY-FIVE

Holly: Warthogs and Weasels

When Holly arrived with Cat a few minutes later, she was surprised to find Belle in the rehearsal room with Bianca and Mayu.

'I just got here,' Belle grumbled, 'and found these two. Apparently they just felt like doing some singing practice!'

'No law against it, is there?' snapped Bianca. 'Or do we have to ask permission from your precious band if we want to sing now?'

'But we booked this room days ago,' Holly explained.

'Well, try telling your friend Mrs Butterworth that! She didn't seem to think it was booked when I spoke to her this morning.' Bianca's laugh was as cold as water dripping from an icicle.

Cat, on the other hand, looked as if she were about to erupt. She threw down her bag and stormed across the room. Holly opened her mouth to remind Cat to *rise above it*, but it was too late for that now. Far too late!

She could almost see the molten lava bubbling under Cat's flame-red hair.

'Bianca!' she yelled. 'You knew perfectly well we'd booked this room. You heard us talking about it this morning. You're a mean, selfish . . . *warthog*.'

Warthog? Holly thought. *Where did that come from?*

'Ooo-ooh! Temper, temper!' Mayu mocked in her sickly sweet voice.

'And you're just as bad, Mayu!' Belle said, striding over to stand shoulder to shoulder with Cat. Her voice was level but she was quivering with rage. 'You've done this deliberately to mess up our chances in the competition. You, you . . .'

'. . . *weasel!*' Cat shouted.

'OK,' Holly said, trying to calm the situation. 'Maybe there's another rehearsal room available . . .'

'No, this was the last one free when I booked it,' Belle seethed.

The door banged open and Holly turned to see Nick Taggart.

' 'Allo, 'allo, 'allo, what's going on 'ere then?' Nick barked in a comedy-policeman voice. He pretended to lick a pencil stub and write something down in a notebook. 'I was proceeding along the corridor in a northerly direction when I thought I 'eard a *disturbance* in rehearsal room two.'

Bianca and Mayu rolled their eyes.

'What seems to be the problem 'ere, then, madam?' Nick asked.

This is so not helping! Holly thought. She waited for Belle to put Nick in his place – or rather the place that Belle *thought* was his; like, maybe the recycling bins behind the kitchen. But to her astonishment, Belle looked at him as gratefully as if he really *were* a police officer arriving on the scene of a crime!

'Bianca and Mayu *say* they booked this room first,' she blurted out.

Nick grinned and nodded slowly. Holly could almost see the lightbulb flash on above his head as something clicked. 'Are you feeling any better now, Belle?' he asked, dropping the policeman act.

Belle frowned. 'Why does everyone keep asking me how I am today?'

'Why don't you ask Bianca?' Nick said pointedly.

Bianca's mouth was trying to move in several different directions at once, but no words came out. She jabbed at random buttons on the sound desk.

'OK, *I'll* tell you, Belle!' Nick said, grinning. 'I happened to be in Mrs B's office this morning when she got a phone call. Not that I'm *nosy* of course, but – the caller said that Belle was ill and could they book rehearsal room two instead. I assumed it was Holly or Cat, but just maybe it was someone else . . .'

Everyone stared at Bianca. Her mouth was now firmly stuck in gulping-goldfish mode. 'Whatever!' she spat finally. Then she stood up, grabbed her bag and flounced off, 'accidentally' barging into both Belle and Cat as she passed. Mayu sidled out after her.

'Grr!' Cat growled. 'Those two! Mean, devious, treacherous little . . .'

'. . . *warthogs?*' Holly suggested.

Belle giggled. 'But did you see the look on Bianca's face when Nick caught her out?'

Holly leaned back against the wall and sank to the floor. Within a few moments all four of them were helpless with laughter.

'That was brilliant, Nick!' said Cat. 'You're a star!'

Nick grinned at her. 'All in a day's work! Hey, can I stay and see how you're getting on?'

'Er, I don't know . . .' Holly stalled. She didn't mind, but she was sure Belle wouldn't want Nick sitting in on their rehearsal.

But, 'Sure,' Belle told him. 'If it's OK with you two?

Nick could give us some useful feedback. You know, on the technical side . . .'

Holly looked at Belle in amazement. If she didn't know better, she'd *almost* think that Belle was growing quite fond of Nick!

'We'll take all the help we can get!' Cat said gratefully.

'I would be honoured to give you the benefit of my valuable opinion!' Nick settled himself into a chair by the sound desk. 'When you're ready, girls. From the top!' he said, clapping his hands.

'I'm beginning to regret this,' Belle muttered.

When Holly, Cat and Belle finished performing *Done Looking!* Nick applauded enthusiastically. 'Great song! It's so feel-good, and the dance routine really works.'

'Thanks,' Holly said, delighted with this reaction to her work.

'Cat's energy was great,' he added. 'And Belle, you were amazing. Your voice was perfect.'

Belle smiled broadly and pulled up a chair next to him. 'We were wondering about putting an extra chorus in the middle . . .'

Nick nodded. 'Good idea. I can edit the backing CD for you. And you know what I think might really work? How about doing one verse in Spanish for a real Latin flavour?'

'That'd be great,' Holly said, 'but does anyone speak Spanish? I don't.'

'Nor me, but I could ask Nathan to do a translation and then teach us how to pronounce it?' Cat offered, her eyes twinkling with excitement.

'Awesome!' exclaimed Belle.

Holly smiled. It seemed they were becoming Nick's Angels after all! But he was being so mega-helpful that no one was objecting now.

'Which one of you is the songwriter, anyway?' Nick asked. 'Or is it a joint effort?'

Holly exchanged *should-we-tell-him?* glances with Cat and Belle. 'Oh, why not?' Belle said, speaking for all of them.

So, as they packed their stuff away, the girls gave Nick an abridged version of the Mystery of the Secret Songwriter, leaving out a few minor details – like the fact that Nick himself had been one of their prime suspects. 'But we still have *no idea* who N.A. is!' Belle concluded.

'Hm . . . N.A. . . .' Nick murmured thoughtfully. 'Maybe they're not the writer's initials at all. N.A. stands for Not Applicable – you know, like when a form asks how many times you've been married or had the bubonic plague or something.'

'So, if the letters N.A. *aren't* initials, the writer could be *absolutely anyone* . . .' Cat said slowly.

'*Oh, no!*' Holly gasped, suddenly realizing that this was a *catastrophe*. 'We've only gone and filled in *Songwriter: Not Applicable* on our entry form!'

'Mr Garcia's going to think we're total head cases!' Cat groaned.

'What are we going to do?' Belle said despairingly. 'They'll definitely disqualify us from the talent competition now!'

Holly stared at Belle and Cat, seeing her own rising panic reflected in their eyes.

'Not necessarily,' Nick said in a reassuring tone. 'Wait and see. People probably make mistakes on their forms all the time. They'll get in touch with you if there's a problem.'

Holly looked gratefully at Nick. She really wanted to believe him.

'OK,' Cat said. 'We'll just have to hope for the best.'

Holly jumped as the bell suddenly rang for afternoon lessons. As she picked up her bag, her emotions were whirling around like a kaleidoscope. They just *couldn't* be thrown out of the talent competition now, could they?

CHAPTER TWENTY-SIX

Holly: Burning Ears and Smiling Eyes

A few minutes later, Holly trooped into Mr Grampian's acting class with Nick, Cat and Belle. They were in one of the larger performance spaces, but the room still seemed more crowded than usual.

'Welcome, fellow thespians!' Hawk-man proclaimed. 'Today, my esteemed Year Eight students, we are joining forces with the *crème de la crème* of Year Ten in a combined exploration of the dramatic arts . . .'

As he spoke, Holly was still worrying about the talent competition. Her attention wandered to the group of older students sitting at the back. She recognized several faces – Lucy Cheng, Felix Baddeley and . . .

. . . Ethan Reed!

Holly instantly felt a blaze of heat engulf her ears. She shuffled her chair so that she was out of sight behind Cat. *Holly Jasmine Devenish*, she reprimanded herself, *just grow up!*

This thing with the burning ears happened every time she saw Ethan. Which was quite often since she'd started going swimming several times a week. She knew that Ethan liked her. He always smiled and chatted about his training schedule. But he obviously only liked her as a friend.

And I like him as a friend too, Holly told herself.

She peeped out. Ethan was leaning over to talk to someone. The corners of his eyes did a kind of smiling-thing that made her heart do a little dance – even though he wasn't even smiling at *her*.

OK, I like him as more than a friend! Holly finally admitted it to herself. But what chance did she have? He was Mr Super-Popular-Good-Looking-Year-Ten-Guy, and she was . . . well, she was just Holly. She would be a laughing-stock if she told anyone about it. *Just keep quiet and get over it*, she told herself.

'Can you see all right back there, Hols?' Cat asked.

'Oh, er, yeah, fine, thanks,' Holly mumbled, tuning back in to the class.

The Year Ten students, Mr Grampian explained, had written one-act plays, and were now going to work on their directing skills by acting them out with the help of the Year Eight students. They would spend the first hour rehearsing the plays. They would then perform them to the class so they could all evaluate each other's acting and directing. He started to read through the groups of students that would be working together. Ethan Reed was the first name called out.

'Ah yes, Ethan – you're working with Nathan Almeida, Serena Quereshi and Holly Devenish.'

Holly's ears burned once again.

CHAPTER TWENTY-SEVEN

Cat: Secret Love and Other Mysteries

'Next, Duncan Gillespie,' Mr Grampian continued. 'And your chosen few are Nick Taggart, Mason Lee and Catrin Wickham.'

Cat and the rest of her group pulled up a circle of chairs. Duncan was a tall gangly boy with thick dark hair swept forward as if he were standing in a wind tunnel. He talked the group through his play as he handed out scripts. 'It's about a sweet old lady called Mrs Stanley,' he said. 'That's you, Cat. But she leads a secret double-life as a blackmailer.'

Cat soon forgot all her worries about the talent competition as she immersed herself in her character. Mildred Stanley was a complex part, and she loved the challenge. She was blissfully happy as she worked, discussing the dialogue and the best way to bring out the tensions between her character and her husband and her grandson – played by Mason and Nick.

Cat's group was first to get up on the stage. The play

went brilliantly: she delivered her final line, '*I'm off to Las Vegas on the next plane!*' to rapturous applause.

'Magnificent!' Mr Grampian declared as the actors took their bows.

'Thanks, Cat.' Duncan grinned. 'You really brought Mildred to life for me.'

Cat smiled back. 'No problem! She's a great character – although I wouldn't like to meet her!'

Elated, she settled down to watch the other groups. Lucy Cheng, Bianca, Lettie and Zak were next, performing Lucy's play about a group of friends at an audition for a quiz show—

Audition!

Hearing that word, Cat's brain suddenly skidded off-track into a tailspin of worry. She'd been trying to put the *Macbeth* audition out of her mind and concentrate on the talent competition, but now both were only a few days away. She was used to pre-audition nerves, of course; she'd done hundreds of auditions before. But she hadn't been able to spend nearly enough time rehearsing her Second Witch. Time! It seemed to be in short supply these days. Except in Mrs Salmon's science lessons, where every minute seemed to last longer than the one before—

Suddenly Cat was aware that something was going

on. While she'd been contemplating the deep philosophical concept of Time, the next play had started. Ethan Reed was on stage with Holly, Nathan and Serena. The play was a wartime romance. A prisoner of war, played by Ethan himself, seemed to be falling in love with the prison commandant's daughter, played by Holly. Nathan and Serena were excellent as the cruel commandant and his down-trodden wife. Cat nibbled her fingernails, nervous on Holly's behalf. She knew how insecure Holly was about acting.

But her concern was soon replaced with amazement. *Holly was brilliant!* Each time Ethan glanced at her, she blushed and turned away, but then looked back with a sad, yearning expression. She perfectly captured the anguish of secret love. Ethan and Holly portrayed the doomed relationship so beautifully that when Ethan's character was transferred to another prison camp, Cat felt tears running down her face.

Mr Grampian blew his hawkish nose into a silk handkerchief. 'Profoundly moving!' he sniffled. 'Captivating!'

When did Holly turn into a spellbinding actress? Cat marvelled. *Has she secretly mind-morphed with Kate Winslet?*

'I never knew Holly could act like that!' Belle whispered.

'Nor did I!' Cat mouthed back.

But then she remembered how often Holly had been going swimming lately. And of course she'd heard about the diving-into-Ethan's-arms-on-the-steps incident. The whole school had heard about that! And it made her wonder . . . *Maybe Holly hadn't been acting at all.*

After the acting class, Cat felt restless and unable to face settling down to her mountain of homework. She suggested to Holly and Belle that they play some tennis to take their minds off the talent competition.

'So why the big secret, Hols?' Cat asked as they strolled towards the school tennis courts in the mellow late-afternoon sunshine.

'What do you mean?' Holly asked, dropping the tennis ball she was trying to balance on her racket.

'You and Ethan!' Belle smiled. ''Fess up!'

'There's nothing to confess,' Holly said quietly.

'Oh, fine, so you won't be interested to know then . . .' Cat said slowly.

'Know what?' Holly asked.

'Just that Ethan obviously really fancies you!' she replied. 'The way he kept looking at you, it was so sweet!'

'Really? Do you think so?' Holly asked eagerly. Then she stopped herself and blushed.

Cat smiled to herself. *How easy was that?*

'Oh, so you *do* like him then?' Belle asked.

'Well, maybe a bit, I suppose,' Holly admitted reluctantly. 'Oh, OK, I *really* like him. But it's pointless – he's way out of my league.'

'Don't put yourself down, Holly,' Belle said seriously. 'Cat's right, he *was* looking at you. If you asked him out, I'm sure he'd say yes.'

'Ask him out?' Holly squawked. 'Are you *insane*? I can't even *talk* to him without turning into a jellyfish! Oh, look, there's Gemma,' she added, changing the subject. 'Let's ask her if she wants to come and play doubles.'

Cat waved Gemma over.

'Don't say anything about Ethan, will you?' Holly whispered as Gemma trotted over to join them. 'I'm really glad I've told you guys, but that's enough True Confessions for one day!'

'We promise!' Cat said with a grin.

CHAPTER TWENTY-EIGHT

Belle: Shopping, But Not As We Know It

If shopping were a martial art, Belle would be a black belt. She'd shopped for Christian Dior jackets in Beverley Hills, Versace boots in Milan and bought her Louis Vuitton luggage in Paris.

So, on Saturday morning – the day before the talent competition – when Cat and Holly suggested they go shopping for outfits for their performance, Belle *assumed* they'd be hopping into a taxi and heading for Knightsbridge. She *loved* Harrods and Harvey Nicks.

She didn't expect to be sitting on a double-decker bus that was crawling through the bustling London streets towards Camden Market. Markets were places for buying fruit and vegetables, weren't they?

But she was so happy she didn't mind where they were going! All week the girls had lived in dread of hearing news that they'd been disqualified from the talent competition because they hadn't provided the songwriter's name on their entry form. But when the letter from Mr Garcia had finally arrived, it was simply a confirmation of their place in the competition. Belle, Cat and Holly had practically fainted with relief!

They hadn't been disqualified! At last it was really happening!

'You can get *anything* in Camden Market,' Holly was saying. 'I'm sure we'll find something with a Latin American look to go with the song.'

'But not like that frilly frou-frou stuff they wear for ballroom dancing,' Cat insisted. 'We want something a bit edgy.'

Belle looked down at her white Italian-cut jeans and Chanel coat-dress. Then she glanced at Holly, who was wearing a Billabong hoodie and a short checked skirt, and at Cat, in her black leather jacket and glittery silver mini-dress. They all looked so different – would they ever find anything they agreed on?

'Here we are. Come on!' Holly shouted, jumping up excitedly.

'I love this place!' Cat grinned as she clattered down the stairs after her.

Belle followed Cat and Holly along Chalk Farm Road into the Stables Market. They elbowed their way through crowds of shoppers and tourists, all rummaging through the goods piled on the stalls: crafts, jewellery, hot dogs, piercings, saris, CDs – and lots and lots of clothes. It was fun, in a manic kind of a way, Belle thought. *But there are no proper changing rooms! No assistants to bring you different sizes!*

'Come on,' Cat said, darting towards a huge stall of vintage clothing. She burrowed in and pulled out a spangled red flamenco dress with two layers of ruffles. 'Perfect!' she cried. 'And look – with these shoes—'

'Hang on, what about this one?' Holly said, pulling a pink puffball skirt off a rack.

'I am *not* wearing that!' Belle winced as Cat held out a floaty blue and purple dress with a feather trim. 'I'd look like a demented peacock!'

'Oops, this skirt's way too big.' Holly giggled as she pulled it on over her jeans and it immediately dropped round her ankles.

'Oh, no, this dress has a stain all down the front.' Cat sighed. 'It looks like engine oil.'

Belle stared, trying to imagine *who* would work on their car engine in a red flamenco dress.

This wasn't shopping as she knew it!

Two hours later, they still hadn't purchased a thing.

'Anyway,' Belle sighed as they sank down at a table

outside a small café and ordered frappuccinos. '*Matching* outfits would be better. Then we'd really look like a band.'

'That's true,' Cat agreed.

'Maybe we should go to Oxford Street instead,' Holly suggested.

'But it would cost a fortune,' Cat moaned.

'I've got it!' Belle announced, suddenly thinking of a fabulous plan. She whipped her mobile phone out of her handbag. 'Desperate times call for desperate measures!'

'What are you doing?' Holly asked.

'Something I vowed I would never do,' Belle answered with a grin. 'Using my parents' contacts to further my career!'

Cat and Holly gazed, wide-eyed with curiosity and admiration, as Belle got through to her mother. Zoe Fairweather was about to step out onto a catwalk in Rome, but she had time to give Belle the number she asked for: 'Yes, call Pixie Ormolu, darling. She's the best fashion stylist in London; works with *all* the top magazines – tell her I sent you . . . Oh, and good luck with the competition. Got to go, I'm being called!'

One more call and Belle had arranged an

appointment with Pixie Ormolu at her warehouse in Covent Garden. 'OK, we're doing this *my* way now!' she insisted. '*Taxi!*' she yelled, stepping out into the street and waving her Prada handbag in the air.

Pixie Ormolu worked miracles. The tiny woman with spiky bleached blonde hair, pillar-box-red lipstick and oversized black-framed glasses greeted the girls with hugs and kisses.

'Zoe Fairweather is one of my absolute *favourite* clients!' she trilled. She showed the girls into a spacious changing room with wall-to-wall mirrors. Then she flitted around like a humming bird, fetching garments from the miles of racks that ran the length of the building. Within an hour Belle was wearing an elegant silver dress with three narrow frills of black velvet across the skirt. Cat had a fitted black velvet dress with silver ruffles round a plunging neckline that showed off her curves, while Holly wore a short geometric-print silver and black dress. Belle admired their reflections in the mirror.

They looked like superstars!

They held hands and jumped up in the asymmetric leap that ended each chorus of *Done Looking!*

'Just, er, checking that there's enough room for

movement in these dresses!' Belle explained, seeing Pixie's puzzled look.

'Got to fly, girls!' Pixie called back as she darted out of the changing room. 'Can't keep my super-models waiting! Just bring the dresses back when you're finished with them. Oh, and good luck!'

Belle felt unbelievably happy as she Cat and Holly walked up the stone steps of the Garrick School and into the entrance hall. They were laden with bags full of their stunning new outfits and accessories. They had the band, they had the song, and now they had the look – it was all lining up perfectly for the competition tomorrow.

'I can't wait!' Holly breathed, as if reading Belle's mind.

'I know,' Cat agreed. 'I bet I won't be able to get to sleep tonight!'

Belle crossed the hall to check the pigeonholes for messages. She pulled out a letter and tore open the envelope with her teeth as she caught up with Holly and Cat on the way upstairs. She was really looking forward to a soak in the bath and a camomile tea . . .

It took her a moment to register what the words on the page were saying. She stopped dead in her tracks.

Her bag fell and slid down the stairs. Feeling as if she might collapse at any moment, Belle read the note out in a small shaky voice:

'*Dear Miss Madison, Miss Devenish and Miss Wickham,*
Please come to my office at 9.30 tomorrow morning with respect to an urgent matter concerning your entry for the Garrick talent competition.
Yours sincerely, James Fortune (Principal).'

CHAPTER TWENTY-NINE

Cat: Girl-size Tears and Man-size Tissues

At 9.25 the next morning Cat stood outside the principal's office with Belle and Holly.

It was competition day! None of them had slept much, but it was out of worry, not excitement.

We can't prove that our song is original material.

They'll think we were trying to cheat.

We're going to be thrown out of the competition . . .

These thoughts had been revolving around Cat's head all night, like abandoned suitcases on a baggage-reclaim conveyor belt.

Belle was pale, with violet rings under her eyes, and even Holly's beautiful brown skin was more cold tea than caramel this morning. Cat could feel an angry mob of spots threatening to break out on her chin.

'Ready?' she asked. Belle and Holly nodded grimly. With a weight in her stomach like a sack of wet cement, Cat knocked.

'Come in!'

Cat pushed open the door. Originally the old library, the principal's office was carpeted with oriental rugs and lined with burnished oak shelves of leather-bound books. Mr Fortune sat behind an antique desk with Mr Garcia standing beside him.

'Ah, excellent – sit down, sit down,' Mr Fortune said, indicating a row of three chairs.

'Now, Mr Garcia,' Mr Fortune said. 'If you would be good enough to explain the situation to our young friends . . .'

Light flooded in through the sash window and bounced off the polished desk and Mr Garcia's head. 'Yes, certainly, Principal,' he replied. 'As you know, it is a rule of the talent competition that all entrants must perform *original material,* and must list the writer or composer on the entry form. Naturally we assumed that the initials N.A. on your form' – he paused and tapped the piece of paper in his hand – 'were an abbreviation of Nobody's Angels; indicating that your song was jointly written by members of the band—'

'However,' Mr Fortune interrupted, 'yesterday we received information that this was not the case – that you are *not* the writers of the song and, more importantly, that *you do not know who the writer is . . .'*

No prizes for guessing where that information came from!

Cat thought. *Someone with the initial B, no doubt.* And she wasn't talking about Beyoncé.

Cat couldn't bear it any longer. She had to explain that they weren't cheats. 'It's true! We don't know who wrote our song,' she blurted, 'but we weren't trying to pretend it was written by Nobody's Angels.'

'No,' Holly added. 'And we didn't mean *Not Applicable* either.'

'The song was given to us secretly by someone who only signed themselves N.A.,' Belle said, her voice trembling. 'So that's what we put . . .'

Cat pulled the original song-sheets for *Opposites Attract* and *Done Looking!* out of her bag and slid them across the desk. 'Look – here in the corner. It just says N.A.'

Mr Garcia studied the pages. 'Yes, I see. But we don't believe that you were *deliberately* aiming to deceive us. We just have to know who the writer is, so we can ascertain that they have given permission for you to use their song and—'

So that's it then, Cat thought. *It's all over.*

There was a sobbing sound. She turned to see Belle's blue eyes welling with tears. She put her arm around Belle's shoulder and Holly reached across and took her hand.

'Now, now! No need to despair!' Mr Fortune beamed, passing Belle a box of man-size tissues. 'What Mr Garcia was just about to say was that a few moments ago we had a visit – from a certain songwriter with the initials N.A. – to hand in a signed letter giving permission for Nobody's Angels to perform these songs – although they still wish to remain anonymous.'

There was a long silence.

'So are you saying we *can* enter the competition?' Holly whispered.

'Yes, indeed.' Mr Fortune nodded. 'We simply wished to check that your version of events tallied with N.A.'s story.'

'Please go and arrange a time to rehearse with the backing band later this morning,' Mr Garcia told them with a smile. 'The competition will be starting at six thirty.'

'You could always take a short cut through the kitchen storeroom to save time,' Mr Fortune chuckled, doing his twinkly-eye thing in Cat's direction. 'And good luck!'

'Woo-hoo!' Cat shouted triumphantly as soon as they were out of the principal's office. She grabbed Holly and Belle in a group hug and they all jumped up and down, laughing away the tears.

'Can you believe Bianca sneaked on us like that?' Cat asked.

'Easily!' Holly and Belle giggled.

'Well, it didn't work,' she declared happily. '*Talent competition, here we come!*'

The rehearsal did not go well.

It wasn't the backing band's fault: this consisted of many of the Garrick's most musically gifted students, and the arrangement was excellent. The percussion section, with Mason Lee on drums, was lively and spirited – especially the all-important Latin American claves. The string section, including Lettie Atkins on cello, played with passion and verve.

But when the girls started to sing, their voices were lifeless. The sleepless night, followed by the roller-coaster morning, had sapped every last watt of Girl Power – and left them snappy and hyper-sensitive.

Cat accused Belle of coming in a beat early on the chorus. Belle complained that Cat was singing off-key. Holly was so tense that sometimes when she opened her mouth, nothing came out but a squeak.

And that was before they even tried adding the dance routine.

As they left the theatre, they hardly dared look at each other. It was Cat who finally put it into words. 'We're going to have to do *a whole lot better* than that tonight!' she moaned.

'I know – I'm sorry, I was rubbish,' Holly said, hanging her head sadly.

'It wasn't just you, Holly,' Belle said. 'I sucked too.'

'Hey, I'm sorry too,' Cat sighed. 'We're all just tired. Let's get some rest.'

'Yeah, we'll be amazing tonight,' Holly said bravely, linking arms.

'Awesome!' Belle grinned as she took Cat's other arm.

Cat laughed. '*Auspicious!*'

CHAPTER THIRTY

Belle: Living the Dream

The talent competition was finally underway.

Belle hovered in the wings. The waiting was killing her! She'd peeked out onto the stage several times and caught glimpses of the earlier acts, including Sammy Armitage, a comedian, Meredith Lutz playing jazz piano, and a group of male dancers called Move It! They were all awesome! And they were all older. Nobody's Angels were the only Year Eight act in the competition. For a moment Belle wondered whether this had all been a big mistake.

But they'd worked so hard. They had to give it everything!

Half the acts had already completed their performances. Owen Mitchell and Tabitha Langley were coming to the end of their romantic duet. It was a cute song, but Belle could hardly hear it for the blood pounding in her ears.

Nobody's Angels were up next.

Belle inhaled the dusty fragrance of the thick stage curtains and the heat from the spotlights. Tabitha and Owen were taking a bow. The audience – made up of Garrick staff and students – were clapping enthusiastically.

Belle turned to check that Cat and Holly were right behind her. Cat grinned back with a big thumbs-up sign. She'd recharged her batteries with an afternoon Cat-nap, while Holly had gone for a swim. They both looked spectacular in the outfits they'd selected from Pixie Ormolu's collection. Belle smoothed the front of her silver dress and reminded herself to breathe. She'd been doing yoga all afternoon to centre herself. *Work* with *your nerves*, she told herself. *Use them!*

Mr Fortune was walking up to the microphone. 'And the next act is the youngest in the competition . . .' he began.

Belle adjusted her radio-microphone headset and reached over to straighten Holly's wide satin hairband. She could feel the silver glitter Cat had applied to her cheekbones prickling her skin. She peeped out from behind the curtain and looked down at the panel of judges. She recognized the familiar faces of Mr Garcia, Miss Morgan and two other Garrick teachers. Then she noticed a fifth figure: a tall man in a blue suit and a ridiculous hairpiece.

It was Larry Shapiro, the world-famous vocal coach!

Belle felt as if the universe were holding its breath. Her fragile layer of calm was in danger of shattering. What if she messed up? *She would never be able to live it down*.

Then the world started turning again, aided by a firm push from Cat.

'OK, we're on!' Holly whispered.

'Please welcome . . . Nobody's Angels!' shouted Mr Fortune.

Applause ringing in her ears, Belle took her starting position at centre stage, Cat and Holly on either side of her. They were motionless, chins held high, looking out into the audience as the band began to play. Belle noticed Nathan Almeida and Nick Taggart sitting behind the judges. Then she saw Zak, Frankie, Mason, Gemma, Serena . . . Just about every Year Eight student had come to cheer them on!

The lights dimmed and Belle could now make out the words on the banners they were holding:

ANGELS ROCK
GO, ANGELS, GO!

She smiled. She had so many friends at Superstar High – and they were all rooting for her! Her moment of fear was behind her. Raw excitement took its place.

The music started.

Step, and sway to the left, step and sway to the right . . . Belle counted. *Left arm up, right arm up, spin round and . . . sing . . .*

> '*We're done looking! Now we're leaping!*
> *We won't stay in the shallows . . .*'

Belle felt as if she were flying on a magic carpet! Cat and Holly were right beside her, their voices soaring together, their steps in perfect unison.

At the end of the last chorus . . . '*catch the wave, live our dreams . . .*' they all jumped higher than they'd ever done before. Belle knew they'd given the performance of their lives. The audience was standing up, everyone whooping and waving their banners.

Mr Fortune almost had to *push* them off the stage to make way for the next act. They tumbled into the wings in a blur of laughter, hugs and whispered exclamations.

'I thought my heart was going to burst,' Holly gasped.

'And when I saw Larry Shapiro . . .' Belle added.

'And did you see all the banners?' Cat asked.

'Sshh!' hissed the stage manager. 'If you girls want to natter, go to the dressing room – there are still three acts to go.'

Belle came to her senses and looked around, noticing for the first time the other performers huddled anxiously in the wings.

Now all they could do was wait.

But had they done enough?

Breathe, centre, calm! Belle chanted to herself.

Every minute seemed like a lifetime!

At last the stage manager instructed them to go back on stage with the other acts: Mr Fortune was about to announce the winners.

Belle felt her legs trembling as she stood with her arms around Cat and Holly.

'In third place . . . Sammy Armitage.'

There was a cry of '*Yes!*' and applause as the comedian stepped up to collect his prize.

In second was the dance group, Move It!

'And first place . . .' Mr Fortune shouted.

Belle thought she would never breathe again!

'. . . goes to . . . Tabitha Langley and Owen Mitchell!'

Belle squeezed her eyes tight shut to hold back tears, struggling to keep a dignified smile glued to her face. She'd always known they were unlikely to come in the top three, but she had still *hoped*. She couldn't bear to look at Holly and Cat and see their disappointment. When the principal continued speaking, his words were just meaningless sounds – 'special prize . . . exceptional promise . . . Mr Garcia particularly enjoyed the Spanish verse . . .'

The words began to permeate Belle's brain. She opened her eyes and stared at Mr Fortune. Was he really saying what she thought he was saying?

'Highly Commended,' he continued, 'and a place in the Garrick Gala Charity Showcase goes to . . . Nobody's Angels.'

'*Yesssss!*' There was a blur of shrieking and crying and laughing. Belle couldn't believe it. 'Does he mean us?' she gulped.

'Yes, we've done it!' Cat screamed, squashing her in a giant embrace. Suddenly they were all jumping up and down on the spot and screaming.

'Come on,' Holly said, tugging the other two towards Mr Fortune as the audience applauded wildly.

Belle sniffed and wiped the tears from her eyes. This

was what she had worked for. She really *was* a singer. And it felt great!

She was catching her wave! She was living her dream!

As she hugged Holly goodnight in the corridor outside their rooms later, Belle thought she had never felt so tired in all her life.

Or so happy.

There was only one thing missing. 'I *wish* we knew who N.A. was so we could thank them,' she sighed. 'We couldn't have done it without that song!'

'Into your own rooms now, gals, lickety-split!' Miss Candlemas called as she steamed along the corridor. 'School in the morning – even superstars need their beauty sleep!'

Belle pushed open the door, and immediately noticed an envelope lying on the floor. *It must be another song*, she thought, picking it up and showing it to Cat.

'Hey, Hols,' Cat called as she and Belle stepped back out into the corridor. 'Look at this!'

Holly came out of her room, followed by Bianca, whose face was plastered with thick Shrek-green skin cream. 'I hear you lot somehow managed to scrape a place in the showcase,' she muttered ungraciously as she headed towards the bathroom.

Ignoring her, Belle tore open the envelope and pulled out a slip of paper. It wasn't a song, but it *was* from N.A. Cat and Holly stared at her, open-mouthed, as she read the note aloud.

'*To Belle, Cat and Holly. Congratulations!*
Will meet you at ten thirty tonight in C & B's room.
Love, N.A.'

Belle felt a jolt of excitement. But . . . *it was completely against the rules!*

'N.A.'s a *boy*,' she gasped. 'At least we think he is. We can't just invite a *boy* into our room after lights out. Miss Candlemas will go *ballistic*!'

'Well, *technically* we're not inviting him, are we?' Cat grinned. 'He's invited himself!'

'I'll sneak along at ten fifteen,' Holly whispered, ducking back into her room as Bianca reappeared from the bathroom.

CHAPTER THIRTY-ONE

Cat: She'll Be Wearing Pink Pyjamas!

Ten thirty?

That was *way* past lights out!

So it was risky enough that a dressing-gown-clad Holly was in their room, let alone that they were about to be visited by a Mysterious Stranger who was almost certainly a *boy*!

It's just like St Trinian's! Cat thought excitedly. *We could have a midnight feast next!*

Belle, on the other hand, was beside herself with worry: she insisted that she and Cat sit on their beds, ready to pretend to be asleep if Miss Candlemas should call in. She'd also arranged a pile of laundry in the corner as an emergency hidey-hole for N.A., assuming he actually showed up. Holly was curled up under a heap of cushions at the end of Cat's bed.

And, of course, the lights were all off.

At ten thirty precisely there was a very soft knock at the door.

Cat's heart did a back-flip. She looked at Belle . . .

There it was again.

'Er, I've got to get out of bed to open the door,' Cat whispered.

'Go on then,' Belle answered. 'But be quiet!'

Cat pulled the door open, trying not to let it creak, to find herself looking at . . . a pair of stripy pink pyjamas – which wasn't exactly what she'd been expecting. She lifted her eyes to the visitor's face and realized that it was only Lettie Atkins.

'Oh, hi, Lettie, it's you,' Cat said, feeling disappointed. 'We thought it was—'

'N.A., the songwriter,' Lettie whispered, slipping past her into the room and switching on a small torch. 'I know. It's me!'

'But your initials aren't N.A.!' Belle whispered from her bed.

'*Nicolette* Atkins,' Lettie whispered patiently. 'Lettie is a nickname.'

Cat was speechless. Could the songwriter really be the quiet, serious girl with the cello? She was friends with Bianca for a start! She'd always been part of the Mean Team. Although, now Cat came to think about it, Lettie had never really joined in with Bianca and Mayu's spiteful shenanigans. She just kind of tagged along.

'But why?' Holly asked. 'I mean, thank you so much, we *love* the songs, but why give them to us?' She moved over to make room for Lettie among the cushions on Cat's bed. Cat got back under her duvet and Belle came over to sit on the bed too.

'I've always loved writing songs,' Lettie explained, 'but I don't have a very good singing voice. And I'd rather be playing in the orchestra anyway. When I saw you guys at the karaoke party, you had such a great sound – and then I heard you saying you needed an original song for the talent competition, and I just *knew* I could write something perfect for you – but I also knew that if Bianca found out, she'd try to stop me helping . . . So I came up with the idea of delivering the songs secretly—'

'Hang on,' Belle interrupted. 'That's impossible! Last Sunday someone tried to deliver a song under our door. But you were in Bianca's room all the time. We saw you there!'

'Not *all* the time. I left Bianca's room to go to the loo – and started sliding the envelope under your door. Then, when I heard all the commotion, I just ran straight back into Bianca's room.'

Lettie was obviously telling the truth. Cat shook her

head. 'But, Lettie, why do you put up with Bianca bossing you around all the time?'

Lettie smiled. 'She's not so bad really. We've been friends since primary school. She's been much worse since we came to the Garrick though. I think she just feels threatened. She was used to being a big fish in a little pond at our old school. Here, *everyone* is super-talented and she's not Queen Bee any more.'

Cat laughed. 'No, she just acts like one!'

And then, suddenly, the door flew open and there was a blinding flash of light.

'Ha! Got you!' shouted Bianca, waving her digital camera triumphantly. 'A *boy* in the bedroom after lights out. Miss Candlemas will be *very* interested in this photo of . . .' Her voice trailed off as her eyes focused. 'Knickers?' she squeaked. 'Knickers! What are *you* doing in here?'

Lettie looked up from the laundry pile, where Belle had pushed her, and removed a sock from her head.

No wonder Lettie dropped 'Nicolette', Cat thought. *Who'd want to go through life being called Knickers?*

'Come in, Bianca,' Holly hissed, 'and join the pyjama party – quickly, before Miss Candlemas hears you.'

'I don't *think* we've left any boys lying around in here.' Cat pretended to check under her desk and behind the curtains. 'Is this a random spot-check, or did you select our room specially?'

'But . . . but . . .' Bianca was spluttering, 'I *heard* you! I know all about your so-called Mystery Songwriter. You got that note. You were planning to meet him in here tonight.' Then a sly smile stole across her face. 'Oh, so he's stood you up then, has he?'

There was a long pause as Cat exchanged glances with Holly and Belle in the light of the torch and the pale moonlight filtering through the curtains. None of them wanted to give Lettie away.

'I'm starting to think you've been making this whole secret songwriter thing up,' Bianca went on. 'Just to get attention.'

'It's me, actually. *I'm* the songwriter,' Lettie piped up nervously.

Bianca stared in disbelief. 'Knick . . . Lettie . . . What . . . ? How . . . ?'

'Look, Bianca,' Lettie said, 'we've known each other a long time. Ever since I had to hold your hand in reception class because you were scared of Father Christmas . . .' She paused, then continued in an increasingly confident voice, 'I like being your friend, but it doesn't mean I have to do everything you say. I wanted to write songs for Belle, Cat and Holly, so

I did. If you don't like it, fine, but don't make a fuss!'

All eyes were now fixed on Bianca. Everyone kept very still – as if she were a cornered pit bull that might attack at any moment. But Bianca suddenly caved in like a hot-air balloon when the burner is switched off. 'Well, you'll still be in loads of trouble,' she said, pouting, 'if Miss Candlemas finds out you're running around after lights out.' Then she seemed to perk up a little as the realization dawned. 'So you'd better do what I say if you don't want her to hear about it,' she concluded triumphantly.

'Like what?' Belle asked.

There was a long pause as Bianca thought about this. Her face contorted as if she were having an argument with herself. 'I want Lettie to be my room-mate,' she announced finally. 'Holly, you have to swap.'

And, with that, she marched out.

Cat, Holly, Belle and Lettie all looked at each other, then burst out laughing.

'So, would that be OK with you?' Lettie asked Holly. 'I share with Gemma Dalrymple at the moment.'

'It'll be my pleasure.' Holly grinned. 'How about we swap tomorrow?'

'Thanks,' Lettie said. 'Gemma's great, but Bianca and I – we go back such a long way. We're like sisters.

I'm really glad she wants me to be her room-mate.'

Cat laughed. 'This must be a first: Bianca has actually done something that's made everyone happy!'

'She must be sickening for something,' Belle said.

'See, I told you she wasn't *all* bad!' Lettie chuckled.

'Now you guys better go,' Cat said, 'before we really do get caught!'

CHAPTER THIRTY-TWO

Cat: In the Cauldron Boil and Bake

The next morning everyone was tired.

For the first time Cat could remember, Belle slept late and missed her morning run. Then there was a flurry of activity as Lettie and Holly got together with Gemma at breakfast to discuss The Big Swap. Gemma was perfectly happy with the arrangement and they all went off to clear it with Miss Candlemas, who gave them the go-ahead as long as they didn't get the idea that they could 'chop and change willy-nilly!'

At morning break Cat helped Holly to move her things into Gemma's room – fortunately it was only across the corridor. Then she found herself a quiet spot in one of the study rooms and ran through her Second Witch lines for the last time.

The *Macbeth* auditions were at lunch time today!

But, to her surprise, Cat found that she didn't feel panicky about it any more. She was actually looking forward to the audition. She was nervous, of course, but relaxed, somehow. The talent competition had taken her mind off worrying, and the success of Nobody's Angels had really boosted her confidence. She was in control. This multi-tasking business wasn't so hard, after all!

After an even-longer-than-usual science lesson, and then an hour of coastal erosion in geography, Cat and Nathan hurried to the Drama Department. SILENCE PLEASE: AUDITIONS IN PROGRESS said the large sign on the door of the main performance studio. Several other students were already loitering nervously in the corridor, reciting lines to themselves under their breath.

Cat put her ear to the door and heard a voice she recognized as Ethan Reed's, performing one of Banquo's speeches. She checked the schedule and saw that she was due to be called next.

The door opened and Ethan stepped out. He smiled at Cat and nodded for her to go in. Yep, she could see why Holly liked him. Those green eyes and long dark lashes . . .

'Good luck!' Nathan called after her.

Mr Grampian stood up and introduced the other members of the panel. 'Mr Steele is the Garrick's

Shakespeare expert and will be directing the play.' Cat recognized Mr Steele as one of the drama teachers; he returned her smile with a sharp nod and went back to fiddling with his pencil. 'And you have already met the estimable Duncan Gillespie, of course,' Mr Grampian went on. 'Duncan is the assistant director of this production . . .'

Duncan smiled warmly at Cat. She grinned back. This was her lucky day! Duncan had *loved* her portrayal of his character, Mrs Stanley, in the acting class. That *must* be a good sign.

'In your own time, please,' Mr Steele said, gesturing to where Cat should stand in an impatient manner, making it clear that she should, in fact, *get a move on* and certainly *not* in her own time.

Cat climbed up the steps and stood on the stage. She closed her eyes and cleared her mind of Cat Wickham thoughts (*dark eyelashes, the chocolate bar she'd promised herself as a reward*) and replaced them with Second Witch thoughts (*dark, malignant and twisted*).

Cat opened her eyes and stared up at the ceiling as if she were seeing a vision. Then she knelt down and felt around with claw-like hands, as if feeling for objects laid out on the ground. She began in a quiet, sinister voice, rising to a loud cackle as she added the ingredients of her spell.

'*Fillet of a fenny snake, In the cauldron boil and bake . . .*'

At the end of the spell Cat closed her eyes again. Then she fell forward from her kneeling position to lie face-down on the stage. She hadn't planned to end in this melodramatic way, but suddenly all the excitement and emotion of the last few days took its toll and her body just crumpled beneath her.

Slowly she looked up.

The members of the casting panel were all smiling at her.

'Really liked the way you collapsed at the end – like you were drained by the force of the spell,' Duncan said, nodding wisely.

'Thanks,' Cat mumbled, feeling a surge of relief as she stumbled offstage.

'We'll be contacting people about call-backs in a few days,' Mr Steele told her. 'Could you ask the next person to come in?'

Cat wandered out into the corridor in a daze.

'How did it go?' Nathan whispered.

'Really well!' She held up her hands to show her crossed fingers. 'Good luck, Nate!'

Now, where's that jumbo-sized Mars bar? she thought.

* * *

In the afternoon, Mr Garcia's singing class was followed by an extra dance class – tap, with Miss LeClair. Miss Morgan was also there, observing again; the teachers were still trying to identify any extra students to include in the various advanced classes, which would all be starting after the half-term holiday.

Usually Cat enjoyed tap, but the combination of tiredness and Miss Morgan's beady glare meant that she stumbled her way through the lesson like a pantomime horse on automatic pilot.

As she and Holly headed out of the Dance Department, chatting about the audition, Cat realized that Belle had slipped away and gone on ahead. Entering the courtyard, Holly suddenly pulled her back into the doorway. 'Sshh! Look!' she whispered. 'What's Belle up to?'

Cat looked up and saw Belle sitting on one of the benches, still in her dance clothes, talking to Nick Taggart.

'So,' Belle was saying, in a hushed voice, 'you know how all the performers get two free tickets for the Gala Charity Showcase to give to guests?'

'Aye, I do indeed,' Nick answered, in the voice of a rather posh elderly lady from Edinburgh. 'And verrrry nice too. Those tickets are awful expensive to buy.'

'Anyway,' Belle hissed secretively, 'my parents are both overseas. So I wondered if you wanted one of my tickets – otherwise it'll just go to waste . . .'

Cat and Holly looked at each other.

'Aw! Sweet!' Holly exclaimed.

'*What a dork!*' Cat laughed, quoting Belle's first impression of Nick at the welcome speeches.

'I knew Belle was warming up to him *a bit*,' Holly whispered, 'but not this much!'

'It's probably best,' Cat said, 'if Belle never *ever* finds out that we overheard this conversation.'

CHAPTER THIRTY-THREE

Belle: Telling Lies and Matchmaking

Belle wasn't sure what had come over her.

She'd given a showcase ticket to Nick Taggart, of all people! But he *had* helped them with their song, and she knew that it was Nick, along with Nathan, who'd made all the banners and rounded up their fan club of supporters for the talent competition.

And that *still* left her with a spare ticket. Dad was in South Africa filming a new epic movie, and Mom was on a catwalk in Helsinki – or was it Hamburg? There was no chance either of them would interrupt their busy schedules just to come and see her sing. She was on her own. *Hey, girl*, she told herself. *Don't you start feeling sorry for yourself. Now, focus on these math problems.*

It was Wednesday evening. The weather had turned very cold and Belle shivered as she sat in the library with her homework. All the excitement of the talent competition had died down, but the Garrick Gala Charity Showcase was only two days away. They *should* be rehearsing *Opposites Attract* – they had to perform *two* songs in the showcase. But they were having a night off: Belle to catch up on her homework – half-term reports would be coming out any day and she had to make sure that hers was nothing short of perfection – Holly to do some ballet practice and go for a swim, and Cat to play table tennis with Nathan.

Cat and Holly had plenty of people to give their tickets to. Holly was inviting her mum and her old dance teacher, Miss Toft. Her stepdad had volunteered to stay home and babysit her little brother. Cat had a bus-load of family coming from Cambridge (so many that they had bought extra tickets) – Mum, Dad, two brothers, little sister. There was even a granny and an aunt coming over from Dublin.

I can't even find one person to give my last ticket to, Belle sighed. *How sad is that?*

'Hey, Belle, having fun?' Cat laughed as she breezed up behind Belle's desk. 'Thought I'd find you in here. Turns out table tennis is harder than it looks. I'm shattered.'

'Fun? Not really,' Belle replied gloomily.

'OK, I've got two things to cheer you up,' Cat announced. 'One, *Grease* is on telly in half an hour. I've just checked, and the fire's lit in the common room.

So put those books away, get your pyjamas on, and it's you and me for hot chocolates, a huge bowl of popcorn and a good sing-along. Holly's going to join us later.'

'It's a date.' Belle grinned. 'Pyjamas, here I come!' She was ninety per cent cheered up already, and Cat had mentioned *two* things. 'Where is Holly anyway?'

Cat laughed. 'That's the second Reason to Be Cheerful! I've just seen Holly in the sports centre. She was talking to Ethan Reed about backstroke technique or something. Except the way they were looking at each other was *nothing* to do with backstroke; it was all about luuuuurve!'

'Ooh, that's cute,' Belle said, smiling as she remembered how sweet Holly and Ethan had been together in the acting class. She felt ninety-five per cent cheered up now.

'Yeah, but you know how shy Holly is around Ethan,' Cat went on, shooing Belle out of the library as the other students were starting to glare at them. 'They'll probably never get past analysing each other's front-crawl kick!'

Suddenly Belle felt ninety-nine per cent cheered up. 'Hey, Cat, I've just thought of something! I've had a really—'

'Uh-oh, not another of your Awesome Ideas!' Cat said as they trotted downstairs on their way to the common room.

'Yeah! Why don't we send my spare showcase ticket to Ethan and pretend it's from Holly? You know, move things along a bit!'

'Belle Madison!' Cat exclaimed with a shocked expression. 'Are you suggesting we start *telling lies* and *matchmaking?*'

'Sorry, sorry. I just thought . . .' Belle stammered. She suddenly felt hideously embarrassed. Had she crossed some unwritten rule of friendship that she didn't know about? *Just when I thought I was getting the hang of it!* she scolded herself.

'It's the awesomest awesome idea you've ever had!' Cat grinned. '*Let's do it!*'

Belle laughed with relief.

'But don't you need your ticket?' Cat asked.

'No,' Belle said, her laughter suddenly fading. 'I don't have anyone to invite. Not like you – with all your family coming . . .'

Cat smiled. 'Yeah, I can't wait to see them. I've been really missing them. Especially at the beginning of term. I was so homesick.'

'Lucky you,' Belle said. 'I mean, lucky you to have a

home to be homesick *for*. My home is just hotels and stuff.'

'Hey, I've just had an awesome idea of my own!' Cat said. 'Why don't you come home with me for half-term next week instead of slumming it in some five-star luxury hotel?'

'Do you really mean it?' Belle asked.

'Duh! Of course I mean it!'

Belle couldn't believe her luck. She was meant to be staying in a hotel in Paris – where her mother had a fashion shoot – for the half-term week, with some boring old nanny her mum had dragged out of retirement to look after her. Hanging out with Cat and her family in Cambridge would be much more fun. 'I'd *love* to!' she said, returning Cat's bear hug with extra warmth.

She was now, officially, one hundred per cent cheered up.

'Half-term reports, girls, hot off the press!' Mrs Butterworth yelled, scooting across the hall to intercept them as they passed. 'I was just about to put them into pigeonholes.'

With trembling hands, Belle took the large envelope with her name on it. What if she hadn't got the straight As she needed for Dad to let her stay at Superstar

High? She held her breath and ripped open the envelope to get the moment of truth over with as quickly as possible.

She stared in disbelief at the table of results.

Some of them weren't As . . .

. . . at least half of them were A-stars!

Belle couldn't wait to phone her parents and tell them the good news!

'Oh, no!' Cat exclaimed, slapping her hand to her forehead. 'I can't believe it!'

Belle took Cat's report and quickly scanned the page. Cat had been expecting to do badly, but the results were mostly Cs and Bs with a sprinkling of As.

'What's the matter? This looks fine,' Belle asked. 'You got the As you wanted in English and history—'

'But look at this!' Cat groaned, pointing at the B for science. 'No escape from The Fish!'

Belle read the teacher's comment.

Catrin is a bright girl [Mrs Salmon had written] *and produces good work when she can be bothered to do it. I refuse to give her the excuse she wants to give up on science and so I'm placing her in the top set – which I will be teaching.*

Belle laughed. 'Well, you'll just have to work harder at being dim in future!'

Arm in arm, Belle and Cat danced up the main staircase to their room, singing at the tops of their voices.

Now Belle was a hundred and ten per cent cheered up.

Except, of course, as an A-star maths student, she knew there was no such thing as a hundred and ten per cent.

CHAPTER THIRTY-FOUR

Holly: That's What Friends Are For

The annual Garrick School Gala Charity Showcase was a star-studded, larger-than-life event. So large that it was held in the Gielgud Auditorium rather than the Redgrave Theatre. The Gielgud – shared by the Garrick School and one of London's universities – was twice the size. Hundreds of people had bought tickets to see the talented Garrick students, as well as special guest appearances by ex-pupils who were now world-famous superstars.

And today was the day!

With that familiar mixture of terror and excitement ricocheting around her body like balls in a pinball machine, Holly set off for the auditorium with Belle and Cat, taking the short cut across the school grounds. She and Cat were piled high with garment bags containing their outfits. Belle lugged a box stuffed full of make-up, hairbrushes and bottles of mineral water.

The girls hurried through the landscaped park, past

the tennis courts and sports fields, where a football match was about to start. Holly lingered there a moment, watching as Ethan led the Garrick All-Stars onto the pitch.

The dressing rooms were already abuzz with performers getting ready. Holly was starting to unload their garment bags when she heard a high voice warbling, 'Belle! Holly! Cat!' She turned to see Pixie Ormolu, the fashion stylist who'd lent them their outfits. She fluttered in, followed by a procession of three young men in designer jeans. 'My assistants!' she fluted in a flurry of air-kisses. 'Gary is an absolute *genius* with hair, Jean-Luc is my make-up *maestro* – and Terence, well, Terence is *very* good at carrying things.'

Pixie's team set to work, pinning up and straightening, glossing and powdering, while Pixie mostly just talked.

'Your mother asked me to come, Belle, as a personal favour. Zoe was simply *devastated* she couldn't be here, but Giorgio – that's Giorgio Armani, darling – couldn't spare her . . .'

Holly and Cat's reflections grinned back at each other in the mirror: *This was the life! Their own team of personal stylists!* The other Garrick students looked on in curiosity mixed with a dash of envy.

Holly's hair and make-up were the first to be finished and she wandered outside for some fresh air. She perched on a bollard in the car park, trying not to crease her dress. The light was fading from the October evening, and red and gold leaves were rustling in the trees. She could hear the distant shouts of the football match from across the sports field.

Holly took a deep breath as a jolt of adrenaline pulsed through her veins. *Not long now! This is it! Our chance to shine!*

The air was growing chilly and she hurried back to the steamy warmth of the dressing room. Cat and Belle were still sitting in front of the mirrors, chatting. Belle's hair had been pinned into an elaborate twist while Cat's glossy red curls cascaded around her shoulders as Gary, the hair genius, ran the hairdryer over them. The roar of the hairdryer suddenly stopped, leaving Belle's voice to ring out loud and clear: 'I sure hope Ethan got that ticket. He's going to be so happy when he thinks it's from Hol—' She stopped abruptly as she glanced in the mirror and saw Holly standing behind her.

Cat looked round to see why Belle had broken off; the smile died on her lips as she registered Holly's expression.

There was a long, long silence.

'You sent a ticket to Ethan Reed and pretended it was from me?' Holly asked in a low voice.

Belle gulped and nodded. 'We just thought—'

'How could you?' Holly sobbed. She was so distraught, she couldn't say another word. She turned and ran out of the dressing room.

'Holly, come back! The show's starting soon!' Cat called after her.

But Holly didn't stop running. She didn't know where she was going. Her head was a whirl of shock and confusion. All thoughts of the show had vanished. She just wanted to be alone, to disappear. She ran and ran until she stumbled into a small storage room in the basement of the theatre, full of wigs and hats on head-shaped stands. She slumped down in a corner and tried to make sense of what had happened.

How could *Belle and Cat have done this?* she wondered. *They're meant to be my friends! OK, so maybe they* thought *they were being helpful – but now I'm just going to be totally humiliated. Ethan will think I'm a stupid schoolgirl with a pathetic crush on him.*

The door of the storeroom swung open. 'Holly! Are you in here?'

Holly kept very still. There was no way she could

face talking to anyone yet, but a muffled sob escaped her. All at once, Belle and Cat were kneeling beside her, pleading for forgiveness.

'Pleeeeease, Holly,' Belle begged. 'We're so sorry, we didn't mean to hurt you – we knew you liked Ethan and we just wanted to, you know, help things along a bit . . .'

'Some help!' Holly sobbed. 'I'll never be able to face him again! I'll just die of embarrassment. He must think I'm such a sad case—'

'No way,' Cat said sternly. 'Ethan really likes you. I saw it with my own eyes, and my eyes are never wrong. I *know* he'll turn up tonight. You'll see.'

Holly sniffed. A small part of her was so angry she wanted to push Cat and Belle away. *It's too late to say sorry now*, this part said in a mean, whiny voice. She would never forgive them! And she certainly wasn't going to get up on stage and sing with them!

'Holly,' Belle pleaded, 'I know we did a really dumb thing. But remember what you told me in the cab to The Ritz? When I'd quarrelled with Cat?'

Holly shook her head.

'You said, *That's what friends are for – they stick with you even when you do stupid stuff*,' Belle reminded her.

'Stick with us, Hols,' Cat begged. 'We've got a show to do!'

Another part of Holly told her in a kind, firm voice that she would feel *so much better* if she just gave her friends a big hug and apologized for being so silly. This part – which was starting to sound very like her mum – also pointed out that she would regret it for the rest of her life if she threw away her chance of performing with Nobody's Angels tonight.

Luckily this part was much bigger and louder.

'Hurry up then,' Holly said with a weak smile. 'We're on in a few minutes!'

Cat and Belle helped her up and threw their arms around her.

As Holly hugged them back, a very small but quite excited part of her couldn't help wondering, *What if Cat and Belle are right? What if Ethan actually comes to watch me?*

By the time Holly, Belle and Cat had patched up their tear-smudged make-up and found their way backstage to the green room, the stage manager was having a panic-attack. 'Where the hell have you been?' he hyper-ventilated. 'No, don't tell me – you're on in' – he glanced at his watch – 'thirty seconds.' Thrusting wireless headsets in their direction, he frog-marched them to the wings stage right.

'Nobody's Angels!' the celebrity compère was shouting from centre stage. 'Take it away, girls!'

And, with that, Holly found herself dashing onto the stage as the band struck up the introduction to *Done Looking!* At least there was no time to be nervous. It was like diving off the top board. You just closed your eyes and plunged right in!

They were even better than in the talent competition! As she waited for the applause to die down and the music for their second song, *Opposites Attract*, to begin, Holly scanned the front rows of the audience, where the performers' guests were sitting. She spotted her mum, dressed up in her best purple evening dress, and her old dance teacher, Miss Toft, both clapping wildly. The tiny red-haired lady sitting next to her and the girl in the wheelchair must be Cat's mum and her sister, Fiona.

And it was then that Holly realized the face she was really searching for was Ethan Reed's . . .

She found Nick Taggart instead. Holly knew that Nick had one of Belle's tickets. So if Cat and Belle had sent the other ticket to Ethan, he should be in the seat next to Nick . . .

But the next seat was taken by a sun-tanned man in an expensive suit. Holly stared for a moment. To her astonishment, she realized it was Dirk Madison, Belle's father. No one had thought he was coming! Mr Madison caught Holly's eye and waved at her. She smiled back, then nudged Belle and subtly pointed to her father by moving her eyes in his direction. Belle looked shocked, and then delighted.

But Holly felt only a hollow sense of disappointment.

Ethan Reed hadn't shown up.

CHAPTER THIRTY-FIVE

Holly: Congratulations and Celebrations

Holly's heart plummeted.

Of course Ethan hadn't come to see her!

She pictured him throwing the ticket in the bin and then laughing about it with his mates. How could Cat and Belle ever have thought such a stupid idea would work? But it wasn't their fault – she just wasn't the kind of girl Ethan would notice . . .

Holly performed the second song, *Opposites Attract*, with extra feeling. Now she really knew what the song was about. Ethan was her opposite: he was cool and popular and smart and talented – and she was . . . just Holly Devenish. Tears ran down her face as she sang, '*It breaks my heart that we're still poles apart . . .*'

As the song ended, there was an emotionally charged moment of silence, followed by a tidal wave of applause. It was a standing ovation! In spite of her disappointment, Holly couldn't help grinning in amazement and jubilation as she held hands with Cat and Belle and bowed deeply. It was a fabulous moment, and nothing could ruin it for her. Everyone would assume that her tears were tears of joy.

Belle whispered something to the compère, who smiled and nodded. 'We'd like to thank Nicolette Atkins, our songwriter. Without her this would never have been possible,' Belle announced into the microphone, leading a round of applause for Lettie, who sat, blushing, behind her cello in the orchestra pit.

Then Holly ran offstage with Cat and Belle – who were so elated by their success that they chatted and giggled and hugged their way back to the green room, where the performers waited for the other acts to finish. Holly did her best to get caught up in the excitement, but her heart wasn't really in it.

'I can't believe it! My dad actually came to see me sing!' Belle exclaimed, grabbing a bottle of water from the dispenser.

'That's brilliant!' Holly said, as brightly as she could.

Not brightly enough, it seemed, because Cat suddenly noticed that something was wrong. 'What's the matter, Hols?' she asked.

'You were wrong,' Holly sighed, sinking down into a chair. 'Ethan didn't turn up.'

'Well, I'm sure there's a good reason,' Cat told her.

'Maybe he's ill,' Belle added.

'Yeah, right!' Holly snorted. 'He was well enough to play football a couple of hours ago.'

'Just came to say congratulations, girls!' a deep voice boomed. Holly looked up to see Mr Garcia, their singing teacher, striding towards them. 'You were fantastic. A triumph! I'm very proud to have you all in my class!'

And right behind him was Larry Shapiro. Holly watched Belle glowing with uncontained delight as the vocal coach congratulated them – and told Belle how much he admired her voice.

When the two men had left, Belle looked at Cat and Holly with shining eyes. 'This is the best night of my life!' she burst out. Then she clapped her hand over her mouth. 'Ooh! Sorry, Holly – I didn't mean to rub it in!'

Holly managed a smile. 'Hey, don't be silly. Let's enjoy our moment of glory!'

'That's the spirit, Hols!' Cat said, putting her arm round her friend's shoulders. 'Come on – the after-show party's bound to cheer you up!'

As they entered the lavishly decorated reception room, Holly, Cat and Belle were swept up in a whirlwind of congratulations. Holly embraced her mum and Miss

Toft, who were both brimming over with proud *that's-my-girl* smiles. Then she was introduced to Cat's extended family, and watched Fiona, dressed in her frilly party dress, gazing up adoringly as Cat tied balloons to the back of her wheelchair. Meanwhile Belle leaped into her father's arms. 'Dad! You're here!'

'Not every man has a daughter who can get straight As *and* knock 'em dead on stage!' he said, laughing. 'I was lucky there was an empty seat. I thought I was going to have to stand at the back.'

Holly sighed as she thought about who should have been sitting in that empty seat, and then noticed Nick Taggart making a bee-line for Belle.

'This your boyfriend?' Mr Madison asked Belle as Nick hovered at her elbow.

'Oh, no!' Belle laughed dismissively. 'Of course not! He's . . .' Then she paused, and finished, 'Nick's my friend, my *very good* friend.'

Nick beamed as if he'd been awarded the Nobel Prize.

Suddenly Holly noticed that there was music playing. Usually she would have been first out on the dance floor, but she didn't feel like dancing now. Even when Theodora Mackenzie, a senior agent from Star-Makers, the biggest entertainments agency in London, pushed her way through the crowd to congratulate the girls and give them her card, Holly smiled, but on the inside she felt empty. She chatted to Miss Toft for a while, then drifted to the buffet table and picked at a bowl of Twiglets. Cat noticed her alone and hurried over to join her.

Then they spotted Nathan Almeida running towards them brandishing a sheet of paper. *He must have gate-crashed the party*, Holly thought.

'Cat! Cat!' he yelled. 'The call-backs have come through for *Macbeth*. They want me back for Macduff!'

'Brilliant!' Cat said warmly. 'Well done, Nate.'

'But I'm afraid they don't want you back for Second Witch,' Nathan went on glumly.

Cat swallowed hard. Holly knew that she was devastated, even though she was trying to put on a brave face. She was about to give her friend a commiserating hug, when suddenly Nathan was shouting, 'They want you to try out for Lady Macbeth instead!'

For a moment Cat was silent. Then she screamed, 'But that's the *lead female role*!'

Nathan nodded. And then Cat seized him by the hands and hurtled round in a gravity-defying spin.

'Well done, Cat. Congratulations!' Holly and Belle

yelled as other guests stepped swiftly aside to avoid being bowled over by Cat's victory dance.

'Come here, you,' Cat said when they finally came to a stop. She eased Nathan's glasses off his nose. 'This is something I've wanted to do for a long time.'

'She's going to kiss him!' Holly heard Belle gasp. 'I don't believe it!'

But Cat simply swept Nathan's fringe out of his eyes. 'That looks better,' she said with a grin. 'And, Nate, don't ever do that to me again!' she added, swatting his shoulder.

Holly smiled, pleased by Cat's success but feeling a little flat. She knew she *should* be feeling great: her half-term report and grades had been really good, her two best friends were happy, and Nobody's Angels had just brought the house down – what more could she ask for?

She was half listening to Cat and Belle re-living the evening's performance when there was a commotion near the door. An enormous bouquet of white roses was stumbling into the room.

'I'm looking for Holly Devenish,' the roses panted.

Holly looked closer. Beneath the bouquet was Ethan Reed. He was wearing a tuxedo over a muddy football shirt. She stared, completely unable to speak or move.

'I think he means you,' Belle said quietly.

'Unless there's another Holly Devenish in the room,' Cat added, grinning and giving Holly a gentle shove.

In a zombie-like trance, she walked towards the roses.

'Holly, I'm so sorry I'm late,' Ethan said, hurrying over to her. 'I've come straight from the hospital – had to borrow the jacket from a doorman.'

'Hospital? Are you all right?' Holly asked, horrified.

'I'm fine. It's Felix! Broke his ankle in a flying tackle! I went with him in the ambulance to casualty. And I couldn't just leave him. He's a pain sometimes, but he's a mate – you know how it is . . .'

'Yeah, I know how it is,' Holly said, hoping the grin spreading across her face wasn't too blatantly idiotic.

'I wouldn't mind but he gave away a penalty!' Ethan grinned. 'Anyway, thanks for inviting me,' he added. 'You look beautiful . . . Oh, and these are for you.'

'Thank you!' Holly murmured as she took the flowers.

Surely Ethan must be able to hear my heart pounding like a pneumatic drill! she thought. But she didn't care. She just felt euphoric. *Ethan didn't throw the ticket away! He really did like me enough to come to the show!* And *bring me roses! And did he really say I was* beautiful? It was all too much to take in!

She was vaguely aware of Cat and Belle high-fiving somewhere close by.

Holly looked down at the note attached to the flowers. '*Get well soon?*' she asked.

Ethan bent over to look. 'Oops – hospital shop! Sorry!'

They were very close now. Holly could smell the sweet scent of the roses over a tang of hospital-strength disinfectant.

Ethan was gazing at her with an intense, searching expression. Holly looked back into those sea-green eyes and felt her insides turn to melted chocolate – in a good way, not a five-macaroon-tea-at-The-Ritz kind of way.

It was just like her dream. But without the talking otter.

Suddenly the words, *Don't kiss me, I'm alive!* were dancing in her head.

Ethan leaned closer. He was actually going to kiss her!

There's only one way to stop myself saying something stupid and spoiling this moment, Holly thought. She smiled, closed her eyes and returned Ethan's kiss.

Somewhere in the background, party poppers were exploding. Holly had never felt happier.

Now the celebrations could really begin.

TEN STEPS TO STARDOM!

How *you* can make it as a superstar . . .

There's an old saying: 'Reach for the stars' – and it's so true!

★ Step one – and the most important thing about becoming a superstar – is to aim high and believe in yourself. You'll get there eventually!

★ Watch and learn. From your teachers, your friends, professionals on stage – there's always something new to pick up.

★ Practice makes perfect. It really does! There are times when going through the same vocal exercises or rehearsing the same lines feels boring, but every superstar still does them!

★ Don't always focus on being great at just one thing. It's good to excel in your chosen field, but it helps to be a bit of an all-rounder too. Many of the biggest superstars can act, sing and dance!

★ Make sure you look after yourself – it's important to relax. Every superstar has a day off sometimes!

★ Whatever you're doing, make sure you warm up and down – you don't want to risk getting injured. If you do pick up an injury, even a sore throat, it's important to rest up or you could make something small much worse.

★ Sometimes it's easy to get swept up in superstardom: try and remember to keep your feet on the ground and not forget real, everyday life. Good friends are brilliant for keeping you grounded.

★ Try and keep as fit and healthy as you can. Part of being a superstar is looking as good as possible, so it's important to feel good too. Some lip gloss always helps!

★ Always remember that more than one person goes into making a superstar. Your teachers, parents, friends, wardrobe and lighting teams (to name just a few) are all really, really important. Remember to say thank you!

★ And finally, no matter how nervous you feel inside, don't let anybody see. Hold your head up, push your shoulders back and, most importantly – smile!